ALSO BY LAURA DALEO

Immortal Kiss

Bound by Blood

The Vow

The Vampire Within

Laura Daleo

AUTHOR LAURA DALEO

The Vampire Within is a work of fiction. Names, characters, places, and incidents either are the product of the author's imagination or are used fictitiously. Any resemblance to actual persons living or dead, events, or locales is entirely coincidental.

Published in the United States by Author Laura Daleo, San Diego, California

Print ISBN: 9780997846164
ebook ISBN: 9780997846171

In loving memory of Marguerite Elliott.

Her beautiful light will shine down on us for all of eternity.

CHAPTER 1

I jumped out of bed at the very last second, took a quick shower, threw on some clothes, and raced downstairs.

As my mom nagged me about the time, I shoved a piece of toast in my mouth, washed it down with some OJ, then dashed out the door seconds before the school bus pulled up. As usual, my fellow classmates were taunting the new kid, Roger, and Mr. Gilbert, the bus driver, was yelling out his customary, "Knock it off!" at them. I flopped down in an empty seat at the back of the bus and let out a frustrated groan. *Could my life be any more boring?*

I dragged my feet as I made my way into Mrs. Clark's history class and claimed my usual seat. Whose bright idea was it to make history first period? Staying conscious while Mrs. Clark rambled on about a bunch of dead people who changed the world was nearly impossible. I slid farther down in my chair and was about to initiate full zone-out mode when Sam walked into class.

An electric jolt zapped me upright—I could *smell* her. The scent quickened my pulse and sent my heartbeat skyrocketing. My mouth watered as a feverish hunger growled in the pit of my stomach. It wasn't her perfumed skin or freshly shampooed hair. No, it was musky and unpleasant. It got under my skin, and I found it terribly distracting.

As Sam caught me staring, a proud smirk washed over her face. She tossed her golden-blonde hair over her shoulder and slid her slender body into the wooden desk in front of me, then turned around and locked eyes with me, her smug grin widening.

I couldn't take my eyes off her. Her distracting aroma swiftly traveled up my nose, lighting up my brain. Shivers scurried down my spine, spinning my head...what was that smell?

As Sam tugged playfully on my hair, she whispered, "I've been waiting forever for you to notice me, Brandon." She paused, looking me up and down. "Meet me after class on the front steps."

I didn't hesitate to agree. "Okay."

She winked. "I have a surprise for you."

My stomach flip flopped, and my palms grew sweaty. *Surprise?* I had no idea what she meant, but I sure as hell was gonna find out.

Sam's smell manipulated my brain, blurring Mrs. Clark's words together. Once, I got wasted at one of my parents' Christmas parties. I'd chugged down every half-finished glass of beer, wine, or hard liquor abandoned on the table to the point where my head spun out of control. Sam's scent mimicked that same effect. I wanted to gorge on it, whatever *it* was. The sudden ring of the school bell, announcing the end of first period, snapped me out of the muddled fog.

Sam touched my shoulder and whispered, "You go first, and I'll meet you there."

I obeyed and headed straight for the front steps with my heartbeat throbbing inside my throat.

The breeze carried her fragrance. She was behind me; I knew it. My knees wobbled as I turned around.

Sam was inches from me, batting her eyelashes and smiling. She giggled and seized my trembling hand. "Come with me." She steered me toward the park and away from the vigilant eyes at the school. Within the boundaries of the trees and their interlocking branches, we sat facing each other.

"What's my surprise?" I asked, my breathing speeding up.

"A kiss." She grinned sheepishly, then planted her lips over mine.

That smell of hers hammered at the inner walls of my brain. Every muscle twitched, and heat spread over my skin. I pulled away and blurted out, "What's that smell? It's driving me crazy!"

She flinched, and her cheeks flushed bright red. "You can smell me?"

"Yes."

"I...I don't know what to say. This is so embarrassing." She looked away from me. "I'm on my period," she whispered.

That was it—blood! Rich, dark, delicious blood! Wait, blood? Delicious? Was it? I jammed my fingertips into my temples. Her scent was screwing with my head, but I had to taste her. Cupping her face, I kissed her hard and bit her tongue. Warm, coppery blood spilled into my mouth, bringing to life a slew of delightful shivers.

Her high-pitched squeal struck my eardrums, but I didn't care. Her fluids overpowered all my senses. I swished her blood between my teeth, like mouthwash, before spitting it into the palm of my hand. A thick, gooey, red substance coated my fingers. Its power hypnotized me and...altered me. I hungered after it. My tongue darted out of my mouth and snatched up the blood staining my skin. Upon my virgin swallow, I released the low growl swelling in my throat. Out of the corner of my eye, I caught sight of her. Her face had turned a shade of ghastly white, and her eyes bulged out of their sockets. She opened her mouth wide, blasting out another petrified shriek. It echoed inside my ears, yanking me back to reality. I held my hands up and backed away from her, shaking my head. "I'm so sorry. Please forgive me...I'm so sorry."

She scrambled to her feet, gave my shin a swift kick, and shouted, "Freak!" As she ran away, she threatened, "I'm going to tell everyone what you did. Everyone!"

I wandered the park aimlessly with my thoughts spiraling. *I bit her! Why, why, why? The blood...it made me do it!* My feet stumbled to a grinding halt. Her blood coerced me; I knew it with every ounce of my being. Was that even possible? Was I losing my mind? I had to get away from the school. I grabbed my cell and called my mom.

She picked up on the second ring. "Brandon, why aren't you in class?" Her voice sounded strained. "Is something wrong?"

"I'm sick, Mom." My voice cracked. "P-Please come get me."

"Of course, honey."

"Hurry."

"Ten minutes, if that," she answered in a lulling tone.

"Don't worry."

My shoulders quaked, threatened by a wall of tears building behind my eyelids. For the second time that day, I waited on the front steps of the school, a different person—a person who craved blood—a freak!

As my mom's car turned into the parking lot, I bolted toward it. The car hadn't even come to a complete stop when I yanked on the handle and slid inside.

She gave me a heartfelt look, then immediately placed her hand to my forehead. "No fever, so that's good. How is it you don't feel well?"

Looking into her eyes made me want to bawl like a baby. I looked away, then shuddered. "I ache all over."

Again, she touched my forehead, then each cheek. "I'll make you some soup when we get home." She paused, then added, "Your sister's going to be jealous."

Soup wasn't going to fix my problem, and I certainly couldn't tell my mom I'd bit a girl's tongue. I couldn't tell my sister either. I couldn't tell anyone. I forced a smile and glanced at her. "Soup sounds good. Better make enough for Lindsey or she'll be really jealous."

Her vivacious laugh filled my ears. "You're probably right."

As the car pulled away from the school, the knot twisting my stomach relaxed; though, the gruesome act of biting

Sam was less forgiving. The image was forever etched into my brain. I sank deeper into the seat and shuddered.

My mom glanced at me with a line of concern pinching her forehead. "Are you alright?"

That was the million-dollar question. I heaved a sigh.

"My head's pounding. I just want to lie down."

"Thank goodness we live so close." She shook her head, and her frown deepened. "This came on so sudden. When you dashed out of the house this morning, you were fine."

I shrugged my shoulders. I *was* fine, until Sam changed things. Turning onto our street, she added, "I hate it when my kids get sick."

"I'll be okay." I lied, but my mom needed reassurance.

"Of course, you will."

As my mom pulled into our driveway, I pushed open my door. I didn't even wait for her to kill the car's engine before I was hurrying into the house with large strides, running up the stairs and into my room. I flopped onto my bed and buried my face in my pillow. The sobs I'd been fighting all day gained on me. My eyelids gave way to the mounting pressure behind them, spilling hot tears down my cheeks and drenching the pillowcase. My mom walked in during the height of my waterworks display. I quickly swiped at my face, brushing away the tears before sitting up.

"Brandon, honey, take a sip of 7UP," she said, sitting next to me and handing me a can of soda.

I shoved the soda aside on the nightstand, then latched onto her, letting my tears flow again. "Tell me I'm not a horrible person," I cried.

Her arms came around me in a loving embrace. "Why in the world would you say such a thing?" She cupped my face in the palms of her hands. "You're my prefect 16-year-old son."

My breath hitched inside my chest as I thought of the why. "I don't know. I just...I just need some sleep."

My mom pulled two round, white pills from her sweater pocket, then reached for the 7UP. "Here are two aspirin." She stroked my head, then rose from the bed. "I'll start the soup. Try to rest while it's cooking." She quietly closed the door, leaving me alone.

I washed down the pills and fell back onto the pillows, my gaze drifting toward the ceiling. Sam's horrified face spread across it, and I jerked my eyes away, burying my face into a pillow. *Sam, I'm so sorry.* She'd never forgive me. I couldn't forgive myself. There was no forgiving what I'd done. What kind of person bites another person? A freak, that's who.

A Google search could pinpoint what was wrong with me. I glanced at my laptop resting on my desk and shivered. Bad idea. Searching the internet for reasons why someone craved blood might uncover something far worse.

A rock of fear landed in the pit of my stomach. I bolted into my bathroom and splashed cold water on my face. I caught my reflection in the mirror as I toweled off the clammy sweat and stared hard, searching for the slightest change—same hazel eyes, sandy-brown hair, and dimpled cheeks looked back at me. I didn't see a freak or a monster, just me.

I wandered back to my bed and sank deeper into the pillows. The feather-down cradled me, programming my brain to shut down and summon sleep. My eyelids grew heavy, sliding down over my eyes like curtains. I didn't fight it and drifted off.

The creak of my bedroom door sounded inside my head like an alarm. My eyelids fluttered and slowly opened, my vision coming into focus. My sister stood in the doorway, her schoolbooks tucked under her arm. "What do you want, Lins?"

Lindsey bounced into my room, unloaded her books on my desk before sitting on the edge of it. As she twirled a strand of her brownish-blonde hair around her finger, her big green eyes studied me. "You really sick or just faking?"

What I wouldn't give to be faking the whole mess. I rolled my eyes. "I'm not faking."

She plastered one of those "I don't believe you" looks on her face and heaved a sigh as her shoulders sagged. "I hate high school."

That was so Lindsey; everything was always about her. I leaned against the headboard and folded my arms. "Why?"

"I was so popular in junior high. Everyone knew me or wanted to know me. Now, I'm at the bottom of the fishbowl, like scum. My social status is non-existent."

I couldn't help but smirk. "Social status, really? Lins, you're 14."

She turned her nose up at me. "Like 16's old. Besides, I happen to like being popular." She pouted. "Ninth grade sucks."

"Eleventh grade isn't any easier," I pointed out. "The twelfth graders have all the power."

"Hmph. It just isn't fair." She paused, scrunching her eyebrows together. "Something's really wrong with you, isn't there? You're doing that thing with your forehead."

I swiped a hand across my brow. "What thing?"

"Pulsating the vein in the center of your forehead." She shuddered. "Gross. You always do it when you're stressing out."

I waved her off. Truth be told, though, I was in major stress mode. A whiff of chicken turned my head toward the doorway. Mom entered, carrying a breakfast tray.

"Ready for some soup?" She set the tray of steaming chicken noodle soup, soda crackers, and another can of 7UP next to me on the bed. "I came up earlier, but you were asleep."

I licked my lips. "So ready."

She touched her hand to my forehead. "Still no fever. That's good, honey. Eat your soup and get some rest."

Lindsey leaned in and took a deep breath. "Mom, that smells delish."

"There's plenty more downstairs." She smoothed Lindsey's hair and gave her a smile. "Why don't you join me downstairs for a bowl?"

Lindsey jumped off my bed and scooped up her books.

"Totally." She glanced back at me. "Feel better."

"Thanks, Lins."

"I'll check in on you later," Mom said, then followed Lindsey out of my room and shut the door behind her.

I scarfed down the soup and crackers, then chugged half the can of 7UP. I pushed the tray aside and let out a huge sigh.

Once more, I fell back onto the pillows and closed my eyes.

****

I woke to a dark room. A shaft of moonlight cut through the curtains, stretching across the room and shining right in my face, letting me know it was still night. I rolled over to the opposite side of my bed and pulled the covers over my head, blocking out the light. An empty feeling settled in the pit of my stomach. It wasn't hunger, it was the thought of school. I dreaded staring into Sam's unforgiving eyes, and all the pairs of eyes of the people she'd told. I'd tell her I'd contracted a disease, and maybe I had. The creak of my bedroom door shattered my thoughts. Mom entered and flipped on the light, causing me to flinch. *I can't go to school tomorrow. I just can't.*

"Brandon, how are you feeling?" Mom asked, touching her hand to my forehead for the hundredth time.

Her warm fingers pulsated with thick, rich, tasty blood against my skin. *No, not again!* I jerked away from her and scrambled to the opposite side of the room, sinking to the floor. She hurried after me, a thumping vibration following her. The suffocating hum wrapped around my brain, growing louder and louder. I slammed my hands over my ears and wailed.

"Brandon, what's wrong?" Mom dropped to her knees in front of me, her hands latching onto my arms. "Oh my God, you're shivering."

The thumping was coming from her—her heartbeat! Every crushing thud swelled inside my chest, sucking the air from my lungs. I squished a hand between us and pried her away, but she only clung tighter as she screamed for my dad.

With her cry for help, his footsteps pounded against the carpeted stairs as he rushed to her aid. As my dad charged into my room, the thumping magnified. I sat there, imprisoned on the floor, convulsing with each beat of their hearts. The room grew fuzzy as my vision blurred. Lindsey's panicked squeal filled my ears, then all sound faded away to nothing.

The next time I opened my eyes, I was back in bed. A shaft of light from the hallway penetrated through the opening of my bedroom door, while multiple heartbeats sounded off inside my ears. I rolled over to face the doorway. My mom and Dr. Erickson, our next-door neighbor, stood just outside my room, wearing green hospital scrubs. She must have caught him either going to the hospital or just getting home. They spoke in hushed tones. I couldn't make out every word, but I caught something about oxygen to the brain and low blood pressure.

This wasn't any kind of illness. This was some sick craving for blood, and the second time it had manipulated me.

Would there be more? How far would I go to satisfy the need? Would I resort to violence again? Would I hurt my parents or Lindsey? A thin layer of sweat coated my skin as I twisted the sheets between my clammy fists. "Never!" I shouted.

My mom popped her head in. "I'll be right there, Brandon." She faced Dr. Erickson and squeezed his hands. "John, I can't thank you enough for stopping by and checking on Brandon."

"No need to thank me, Diane, but keep that appointment."

"Yes, of course."

"Good night. Call me anytime." He gave her a nod and went on his way.

She hurried to my bedside, that motherly look of concern tugging at her eyebrows. "Honey, how are you feeling?"

"Tired...weak." *Scared I'm turning into a bloodthirsty monster.*

She patted my hand. "Dr. Erickson reached out to Dr. Stewart. We've got an appointment with him tomorrow morning at nine."

I heaved an exaggerated sigh in protest. "Do I have to go? You know how he is. He'll run every test in the world."

The motherly look intensified. "You gave me and your father, not to mention Lindsey, quite a scare. The subject is not up for debate. You're going." Her face softened, and she planted a kiss on my cheek. "Close those gorgeous hazel eyes and get some rest." She stared at me for several seconds before leaving my side.

As she closed my door, I shuddered. If she knew the truth, she'd haul my ass to the nuthouse instead of the family physician.

Once more, my door opened halfway. Lindsey peeked around the frame. "Can I come in?"

That was a first. She never asked. I must've really freaked her out by fainting. "Yeah, sure."

She approached my bed, stopping inches away. Her face twisted like she was in pain. "You scared me." Her voice was gentle and soft, lacking its usual self-centeredness.

I put on my most thoughtful expression. "I didn't mean to scare you or Mom or Dad. Mom says I've got to go to see Dr. Stewart tomorrow."

"That's probably a good thing. He'll go all test happy and find what's wrong."

I busted out laughing. "That's what I said." I let myself get serious and lowered my voice. "I'm kind of scared. What if there's something wrong with me, something that can't be fixed?"

She nudged my shoulder. "It'll be okay. Don't worry."

"What if it's not?"

She locked her gaze on me. "It *will*. You're my big brother, and I need you."

I cracked a smile. "You mean, you need someone to boss around."

A giggle escaped her and more seemed to struggle to get out before she shook them off and held her chin high. "Not true."

I let out a bemused huff. "Yeah, right. You've been bossing me around since you learned to talk. When we lived in that tiny apartment and had to share a room, you claimed the top bunk and ordered me to sleep on the bottom bunk. Remember?"

She shuddered, then rubbed her arms. "That bedroom was haunted. I'll never forget that girl's voice humming that lullaby. No way was I sleeping on the bottom where she could pop out from under the bed and grab me."

I rolled my eyes and waved her away. "I told you then and I'm telling you now, it was Mom. She was probably standing outside our door, trying to get us to go to sleep."

"That voice had come from inside our room, and it wasn't Mom. It was a ghost," she insisted with a firm nod.

My gaze drifted toward the ceiling as I conjured up the past, then I faced her. "It didn't sound ghostlike or creepy to me. It had more of a calming effect as I remember."

She jutted her chin in my direction. "Maybe for you."

I released a low sigh. "Well, right now, I could use that calming lullaby."

"Everything will be okay," she said again, then hugged me.

I hugged her back and longer than normal before releasing her. "Thanks, Lins. It's late, go back to sleep. I'll be fine."

She searched my eyes. "You're sure?"

I waved her toward the door. "I'm sure."

"Okay." She kept her gaze on me as she backed up into the doorway. A half-smile came to her lips before she closed the door, leaving me alone.

After staring at the ceiling for quite some time, sleep finally took over and Sam entered my dreams. She lay motionless beneath me as I hunched over her like a crazed animal. I'd ripped her apart, limb by limb, my face buried inside her open wounds, guzzling mouthfuls of blood.

My eyelids flew open, and I scurried off my bed, flipping on the light, the nightmare still fresh in my mind. My heartbeat throbbed inside my throat as I skimmed over my room. Familiar surroundings fell into my sightlines: my guitars, rock-n-roll memorabilia, skateboards, and gaming equipment. I wiped the sweat off my forehead, trembling, and sank to the floor. Tears rushed forward and spilled down my cheeks as I feared the significance behind my nightmare.

CHAPTER 2

A nurse with thick glasses resting on her nose called out my name. "Brandon Cass."

Mom looked up from her magazine, offered me an encouraging smile, then shooed me toward the nurse. I heaved a sigh, shoved my hands in my pockets and followed the nurse down a long narrow hallway and into one of many rooms.

She gestured toward the exam table. "Have a seat." She sat in front of a computer, her fingers flying across the keyboard as she asked, "What's the reason for your visit today, Brandon?"

I stared at her, thinking, you don't want to know the real reason. "I fainted last night."

"Just the one time?"

"Yes."

"And prior to last night, any nausea, headache, or fatigue?"

"I did have a headache."

More rapid typing, then she pushed away from the computer and stuck a thermometer under my tongue and a cuff on my arm. "One ten over seventy. That's very good, and your temperature is normal." She handed me a blue robe. "Please get undressed and put this on. You can leave your underwear on. The opening goes in the back. Dr. Stewart should be in shortly."

I pitched my clothes into a vacant chair and hopped onto the exam table, adjusting the flimsy robe. Within 10 minutes, two loud knocks came from the other side of the door. Dr. Stewart entered with a wide grin plastered on his face. "Good morning, Brandon. I heard you had a rough night. How are you feeling today?"

I shrugged. "Okay, I guess."

He pulled a stethoscope from his pocket and pressed it against my back. "Take a deep breath." He moved to the opposite side. "Again." After looking in my ears, eyes, and throat, he stood in front of me with his arms held out wide. "Stand up for me, Brandon, and spread your arms like so, then touch your right hand to your nose and then your left." I breezed right through it.

As he scratched his balding head, he asked, "Have you noticed a shortness of breath lately or any dizziness?"

"No."

"Have you seen shooting lights or dots in your vision?"

"No."

"Any ringing in your ears?"

"Well, not ringing, but thumping."

He pulled his wooly brows together. "Thumping?"

"Yeah."

"Hmm. Have you noticed smelling any strong odors?"

"Kind of."

"Like what?"

"I can't really describe it." I lied. The topic of smelling blood wasn't up for discussion.

"Try."

"Um...I can't."

"Have you been tired, feeling a lack of energy?" he asked, folding his arms.

"No."

"Well..."

Here it comes. Wait for it.

"I want to run some blood tests." He handed me a sheet of paper. "Take this to the lab on the second floor. We'll have the results back in a few days." He gave me a nod and left the room.

I blinked. *That's it?* I got off easy. I threw my clothes on and bolted from the room before he changed his mind. The thump of my mom's heartbeat filled my ears as I neared her. "Gotta go to the lab for tests."

She gave me one of her sympathetic smiles. "Do you want me to come with you?"

"Nah, I'm fine. See you in a few."

"I'll be right here."

I ditched the elevator and trekked up the stairs to the second floor, thankful Dr. Stewart went easy on me. I followed the arrows to the lab and took a seat in the lobby. I clutched my hands in my lap, expecting worst-case scenarios. On the other side of the lab's double doors, a vein was stabbed every minute, so why hadn't I picked up on the scent of blood? Not to mention the fact that I hadn't detected a single heartbeat, other than my mom's, either. Was the whole thing a fluke?

A dark-skinned nurse entered the lobby and called out my name. I followed her through the double doors and into a small room, where she gestured toward a school-like chair, furnished with five glass tubes. As I eased into the seat and offered her my arm, a nervous twitch gripped my forehead. What if I flipped out at the sight of my own blood? The sharp needle pricking my skin didn't give me much time to mull it over. My gaze darted to the clear tube and I held my breath, watching my blood swirl upward, filling the cylinder. Nothing happened: no spike in my pulse, saliva didn't fill my mouth, no lunatic thoughts. I slumped in the chair and released a loud breath.

The nurse touched my arm. "Are you okay?"

"I'm good." *You have no idea how good.*

"We're almost done." The hint of concern in her tone showed she didn't believe me. About 10 seconds later, she taped a bandage around my arm. "All done. You can remove the bandage in about an hour."

"Thank you." I left her with a sense of calm spilling over me. I hadn't freaked out, and that, in my eyes, was an accomplishment. I jogged down the flight of stairs and headed back to my mom. "Hey, Mom."

She glanced up at me, then laid the magazine on the table. "Ready?"

"So ready."

"While you were at the lab, Dr. Stewart came out and spoke with me. Of course, he wants to wait for your lab results, but he says overall, everything looks great." She gave me a big hug.

I stiffened in her arms, praying I wouldn't sense the surge of her blood. Again, no reaction. I laughed out loud, then hugged her back. "And he didn't go all test happy on me either."

She held me at arm's length and grinned. "Well, that's a good thing. Let's go home. I'll fix spaghetti and meatballs tonight, your favorite."

"Sounds good, Mom."

****

On the drive home, I dozed off and dreamt of a beautiful girl with chocolate-brown hair. Sadness clouded her ocean-blue eyes as she roamed the empty halls of my school. The desire to comfort her pushed me toward her. Her image warped, then a bloody, pale Sam lay dead at my feet. I jolted upright, my arms flailing in front me.

My mom squeezed my hand. "Bad dream?"

My heartbeat thundered in my chest as I sat motionless, staring at my mom. "Yes," I whispered. I couldn't tell my mom about Sam, the blood, or what I'd done. I looked away and rested my head on the car window. The white dotted lines below rushed along the street. But I had to talk to Sam and somehow make things right. I had to ask for her forgiveness.

CHAPTER 3

The glaring sun vanished behind a cluster of white clouds, darkening the morning sky. I stood facing the school, my enemy. Hold up, rewind; the school was completely blameless. It was Sam I feared, and everyone she'd told. I inhaled a breath of determination, mentally preparing myself to face her. She'd refuse my apology, but I had to try. Her forgiveness meant everything to me.

I shoved my hands in my pockets and crept along the hallway as the other students sprinted past me, their heartbeats thumping louder than my own. The amplified vibrations fanned across my chest, stealing the air from my lungs. I managed shallow, painful breaths as I fled the horrid sound, escaping inside the classroom.

As the door swung shut behind me, the relentless clatter stayed. I'd trapped myself inside a room full of beating hearts—my classmates' hearts—and done nothing to improve my situation; in fact, I'd worsened it. The delicious coppery scent of their blood rushed into my brain, spinning my head. One by one, they began to mutate into a large, pulsating red mass. Sweat dripped down my forehead and drool seeped out the corner of my mouth as I shuddered at the thought of feasting on their blood.

"Brandon, what's wrong?" Mrs. Clark's voice entered my head, muffled and distant, yet she stood at my side, pressing her blood-filled palm against my cheek. "Are you sick?"

My lips couldn't form a single word. I forced out a low moan in response.

"You're ice cold! I'm taking you to the nurse's office." She turned to Marsha, the class brainiac, and ordered, "Marsha, please lead the class in reading chapter 12. I'll be right back."

As Mrs. Clark ushered me out the door, I glanced back at Sam. Her vindictive hate-filled eyes met mine, and she mouthed the words, "Everyone knows." I slumped against Mrs. Clark. No apology in the world would be good enough for Sam. I was now and forever her enemy.

As I hobbled down the hall with Mrs. Clark, the steady rhythm of her heart pumping out blood I would never taste tormented me. When we reached the nurse's office, she pushed me through the door and shouted, "Nurse Garret, I need your help!"

Nurse Garret's pasty white forehead wrinkled as she latched onto my free arm and pointed to an open doorway. "Help me get him onto the cot."

Together, they shuffled me into the room with a rollaway cot. Mrs. Clark tucked a pillow under my head as she said, "It's going to be okay, Brandon."

Nurse Garret peered at me over the rim of her thick glasses and stuck a thermometer in my mouth. She glanced at Mrs. Clark. "Go back to your kids. Brandon will be okay."

Why did everyone keep saying that? I was far from okay.

Mrs. Clark gave me a brief wave, then left me alone with Nurse Garret.

"Your temperature's normal, and color is coming back to your cheeks. How are you feeling?"

The only heartbeat rattling my brain belonged to Nurse Garret, and my sweating and drooling had eased off, so I guess that was an improvement. "Better. Just a little tired."

She patted my hand. "Do you want to rest here awhile or should I call your mother to pick you up?"

No way. "I'll hang out here a while longer."

"Very well." She retrieved a bottled water from a small refrigerator in the corner and handed it to me. "Drink small sips." She then returned to her desk in the next room.

As I laid there, I came to the conclusion that something utterly foreign had replaced my normal and boring life. How could I detect someone's heartbeat or smell their blood? I wasn't a superhero or gifted with special powers. And why was I so attracted to the scent? Why did it hold such power over me? None of this made sense. Then there was Sam. I'd seen the hostility in her eyes, but I couldn't blame her. She had every right to hate me. There was nothing I could do or say that could change that.

Nurse Garret popped her head in. "Feeling better?"

I offered her a halfhearted smile. "Yes, thank you. I think I'm ready to go back to class."

"Are you sure? You can rest awhile longer if you'd like."

I pushed off the cot and shook my head. "No, I'm ready."

She scribbled something down on a piece of paper and handed it to me. "Take it easy the rest of the day. No physical ed. Give this excuse to your PE teacher."

"Okay. Thank you."

As I trudged along the hallway, skirting Mrs. Clark's class crossed my mind; a face-off with Sam wasn't high on my agenda.

Footsteps rushed up behind me, then I heard my name. Just as I turned my head, a fist slammed into my face. I swayed from the sharp sting swelling underneath my eye. More sneakers slid along the polished floor before a pudgy arm trapped me in a headlock. Someone started shoving me toward the girls' bathroom, and I knew once they got me past that door, nothing good would come of it. Summoning up every ounce of strength in my body, I rooted my feet into the floor and fought back. I might have bought myself an extra minute or two before the bathroom door swung open and they threw me inside. I tripped and came down hard, my head striking the concrete floor. Shooting pain swept across my forehead, then a layer of darkness blurred my vision. I shook off the daze, forcing my eyelids to stay open and struggled to stay alert. At that moment, I caught my reflection in the mirror on the opposite wall. Dark, red blood gushed from a jagged gash over my eyebrow, the eye beneath swollen shut with a nasty purplish-blue bruise.

Gabe, Stevie, Will, Jana, Katie, and Megan—my friends—blocked the doorway, grinning like crazed clowns. Sam stood in front of them, snickering, then a cold, flat glare altered the color of her eyes as she shouted, "Hurt him!"

I blinked, then scrambled to my feet. Gabe charged straight into me, knocking me over, pinning me down with the weight of his body. I squirmed beneath him, sending a knee into his chubby gut. "Sam, I'm sorry," I cried, struggling to free myself. "Don't do this."

"Shut up!" Sam's voice rattled as she screamed. "You don't get to apologize. You get to feel pain...my pain!"

I didn't say another word. My pleas would only fall on deaf ears, but I wasn't going to lay there and let them beat the crap out of me either. I landed a fist into Gabe's side, and a loud grunt flew out of his mouth. He pressed down harder, squishing me like a bug against the cold cement floor, while Stevie, Will, Jana, Katie, and Megan hammered my rib cage with the soles of their shoes. My torso collapsed like a balloon, and crippling spasms forced me to gasp for air. Cold sweat drenched my body, and I swore I was going to throw up. I couldn't even cry out; each new blow stripped me of my voice. I just laid there, helpless, silently praying they'd stop.

As if Sam heard my pleas, she said, "He's had enough. Let him go."

Gabe obeyed her wishes and backed off, and a sudden gush of air flowed back into my lungs. Being able to breathe triggered a release of grateful tears, but I couldn't let them see me cry. I swiped my sleeve across my eyes before trying to sit up. Tucking my legs beneath me sent burning pain ripping through my ribs. I belted out an injured howl, sparking laughter from my attackers.

"Oh, Brandon, my girlfriends and I saved something for you." Her merciless tone told me my punishment wasn't over.

I looked up to see her quivering hands holding a brown paper bag over me. "We collected this very special gift just for you." An ugly grin twisted her mouth as she dumped a pile of bloody tampons over my head.

I flinched, then ducked, flicking away as many as I could.

I glanced to the floor, feeling naked and on display.

"Hey, Brandon, need a tampon?" Will teased.

His smartass tone dredged up something unfamiliar and violent locked deep inside me. I wanted to inflict pain, squeeze the life out of him, make him pay. A surge of adrenaline pushed me to my feet and my fist into Will's gut. I punched him again with a right hook to the jaw. Will staggered into the mirror, hitting his head and smearing the glass with brilliant red. A shiver of pleasure ran down my spine as the ruby fluid called out to me, beckoning me to come have a taste. I didn't hesitate to accept, and I wedged myself between Will and the glass. As my tongue snatched up the gooey blood, my own reflection confronted me. I stumbled backward, my eyes bulging at the stranger in the mirror. *Oh God, what have I done*?

Sam scurried away from me and hid behind Stevie and Gabe. Jana, Katie, and Megan huddled in the corner, clinging to each other and whimpering. Will stood stock-still next to the mirror, his eyes wide and fixed on me. My hands trembled, and so did the rest of my body. *I attacked Will! I craved his blood! I'm a freak!* I bolted from the bathroom, fleeing from the blood I so badly craved.

I inched down the vacant hallway toward the front doors. Everyone was in class, but still, I pulled my hoodie over my bloodied face, not wanting to attract attention. I glanced over my shoulder before slipping out the door and limping toward the bus stop. My house was too far to walk. I'd never make it without collapsing, and calling my mom was out; she'd go ballistic. The longer I could keep her in the dark, the better.

I made it to the bus stop, then sank onto the bench as blood trickled down my face and fell into my lap. I needed a bandage of some kind to apply pressure. The only thing I could think of was my T-shirt. As I stripped off my jacket and shirt, I glanced down at my ribs. My beaten body resembled an abstract painting of blues, purples, and reds, all smeared together. My friends had done this, but what had I done to them? Tears flooded my eyes, and I let them fall as I sat there staring at the ground. Several more drops of blood splattered the sidewalk before I pulled my hoodie back on, then wadded up my T-shirt, pressing it against the gash in my forehead. The instant the cloth rubbed up against the wound, it set off a round of smarting, burning, unbearable pain. I let out a whimper, then clamped my mouth shut, suppressing a scream.

The loud whoosh of air brakes hit my right ear. As the gray and white bus rolled to stop in front of me, a rush of relief burst out of my mouth. My legs shook as I rose off the bench, bent over like an old man, hobbling onto the bus and pulling my hoodie farther down my face. I kept my head lowered as I shoved my money into the slot, then retreated to the back of the bus, away from everyone else.

As the bus driver veered into traffic, he hit a bump in the road, sending a swift jolt into my rib cage. My body caved, then I bit down on my lip, trapping a shriek of pain inside my mouth. That was just the first bump; he managed to find seven more during the 10-minute ride to my street. Drenched in sweat and tears, I pulled on the cord and mumbled, "I'm almost home."

The bus rocked to a stop, and the door swung open. My wobbly legs carried me to the sidewalk where I stood, shaking uncontrollably. I slumped to my knees, just as the bus disappeared around the block. After sucking in several quick breaths, I slowly pushed to my feet, dragging one foot forward, then the other, inching my way home.

As my mom's favorite purple tree shading our house came into view, a huge sob swelled in my throat. I'd never been so happy to see my home. The thought of bending down and kissing our front porch crossed my mind as I snuck inside and quietly closed the door behind me. I wanted to bolt up the staircase and reach the privacy of my room without running into my mom, but I crept along, one stair at a time, again hunched over like an old man.

I'd gotten halfway when she called after me, "Brandon, why aren't you in school?"

Hearing her voice dredged up my childhood when every little scrape, scratch, or cut intensified with pain once my mom was near, and today was no different. The throbbing pain hammering nails into my ribs jumped from a level six to a level 12, sending a grunt flying out of my mouth. Instantly, I scooped an arm around my torso, praying my rib cage wouldn't shatter into a hundred pieces.

"Did you hear me?" She sounded peeved.

I let my bloody T-shirt fall to the floor as I slowly turned to face her. The rosy color drained from her face as she stood completely still, with a hand clamped over her mouth. Seconds later, her paralysis broke and a gasp escaped her lips before she ran to my side. "Dear God, what happened? Who did this?"

I sagged against the wall, bawling out a lie.

"I–I...d–don't...k–know."

Her hands fluttered about her face as she glanced around the room, as if searching for answers. "I'm taking you to the ER," she blurted out, then pointed a finger at me. "Don't move. Have to get my purse. Don't move." She left me on the stairs as she dashed to the second floor, mumbling, "Oh my God, oh my God."

I cringed knowing she'd demand the truth and I'd have to tell her my horrible secret.

CHAPTER 4

The nurse with the chestnut brown hair and light blue eyes, who had taken my vitals in the ER, came and got me from Radiology and wheeled me back to my room. She pulled a syringe filled with clear fluid from her pocket and injected it into my vein. "This will help with the pain."

The medication instantly warped my mind into a hazy fog, and somewhere inside that fog, I found something vaguely familiar about her. As she adjusted my pillow, I gazed up at her, searching her eyes. "Do I know you?" I asked, certain I did.

A kind smile spread across her lips. "We met earlier today. I'm your nurse."

I rested my hand on her arm and pressed, "No, I meant before today."

"You must have me confused with someone else," she replied, placing my hand back on the bed. "It's probably just the medication."

A man with a scruffy red beard, wearing pale green scrubs, popped his head inside the doorway. "Ready for me, Anne?"

She glanced in his direction, then shook her head. "Dr. Erickson hasn't written up the order yet. He's still speaking with his mother."

The bearded man entered anyway, pushing a cart topped with gauze, tape, scissors, and some other doctor-like stuff to the side of the bed. "Hi, Brandon, I'm Brad, the guy who's going to put you back together with a little tape and sutures." A wide grin claimed his face. "Don't worry, you won't feel a thing."

The nurse gave him a sweet smile before facing me.

"You're in good hands with Brad."

Dr. Erickson strode into the room, his broad shoulders tucked into a white coat, with my mom glued to his side, clutching her purse against her chest like a shield. Dr. Erickson handed the nurse a clipboard, then gave a firm nod at the bearded man before focusing on me. He arched his unruly brows as he said, "Brandon, the lacerations on your forehead and lip are fairly deep."

My lip? Had one of them punched it? I had no memory of that at all.

"Both require stitches. The good news is your head CT was normal; however, your chest X-ray revealed three fractured ribs. The fractures will heal with rest and pain medication."

My chin quivered, knowing that my own friends had kicked me so hard, they'd cracked my ribs.

Dr. Erickson gestured toward the bearded man. "Brad will be suturing your lacerations shortly."

The nurse approached my mom and rested her hand on her shoulder. "Don't worry, Mrs. Cass, Brad will take excellent care of your son." Then she left the room.

My mom didn't appear convinced as a deep frown swallowed up her forehead. Her concern would only skyrocket once I confessed the truth, and I had no logical explanation for my sudden blood urges or why they forced me to do gruesome things. Whatever plagued me seemed hell-bent on taking over my life, and I wanted my life back!

Dr. Erickson scribbled something onto a notepad and handed the top sheet to my mom. "Diane, I'm giving Brandon a prescription for codeine. You can get it filled at the hospital pharmacy while he's being treated."

She released one hand from her purse to squeeze mine. "I'll be right back."

"I'm okay, Mom." Was I? I had no idea, but she needed to hear it, so I said it for her.

Her hand trembled slightly over mine as she said, "My brave son."

Dr. Erickson gestured toward the doorway. "Let me show you to the pharmacy."

She waved at me, then vanished down the hallway with Dr. Erickson.

Brad straddled a stool he'd placed by the cart, then snapped on a pair of gloves. "Here we go." He swabbed my lip with a large Q-tip, then grabbed a second one and brushed it across my forehead. "This is numbing cream. It helps take the sting out of the Novocain injection."

"Injection? You mean, inside the wound?"

"Around the site. You'll feel a pinch or two, but it's over quickly. Now, let's get you nice and numb," he said, picking up a large syringe with a hefty needle to match.

Burning pain blazed across my flesh, like a ton of bees stinging at once. My eyes watered, spilling out tears. "A pinch!

Shit...that friggin' hurts."

"Almost finished," he said, inflicting more pain.

I squeezed my eyelids shut and clenched every muscle, waiting for the torture to stop.

"Done. Sorry, I know that was uncomfortable."

I glanced at him, now on my guard. "You're sure I'm not gonna feel the sutures?"

"I'll test the area before I start. If you need more Novocain, just let me know. Sound good?"

I gave a hesitant nod. "I guess so."

As he turned toward the cart, I looked away, wanting no knowledge of what was to come. The ripping of paper and clanging of metal set off an alarm inside my head, stirring the hairs on my arms, yet I kept my gaze fixed on the opposite wall.

"All right, Brandon, I'm going to apply some pressure to your forehead and lip with my finger. Tell me if you feel anything."

"Okay."

"Anything?"

"No."

"How about now?" I shook my head.

"And now?"

"No, nothing."

"That's good. It means the Novocain is working, and we can get started."

"I'm gonna keep my eyes closed if that's okay?"

He chuckled. "That's quite all right."

As he worked on me, there was some tugging and pulling, but no pain. My muscles relaxed, and I sank into the hospital bed. "I'm still good."

"Just finishing up the last couple sutures. Would you like to see before I apply the gauze bandage?"

"I guess."

He handed me a mirror. "Voila!"

I slowly raised the mirror until my reflection came into view. A perfect crisscross line of stitches ran between the puffy, purplish skin of my forehead, and another along the edge of my inflated, angry red upper lip.

He blew on his knuckles. "Pure perfection, wouldn't you say?"

I replied with, "Will I have scars?"

His lips spread into a wide grin as he bandaged my wounds. "Are you kidding me! My work never leaves scars."

I heaved a sigh. "So, can I go home now?"

"That's Dr. Erickson's call, but I'm sure it won't be much longer. Do you want me to wait with you until your mother returns?"

"Nah, I'm good."

He gave my shoulder a squeeze. "You're going to be just fine."

I watched him walk out the door, knowing the word "fine" no longer applied to me. Something had changed me, and when *it* would strike again or what horrible thing *it* would force me to do, I had no idea. My mom and Dr. Erickson returned, stopping just short of the doorway, interrupting my thoughts with their whispering. I picked up on a word or two, but when Dr. Erickson said police, my stomach twisted into knots. Had he called the police? They'd question everything... learn everything. They'd arrest me!

My mom's voice rose to an audible level. "I'm his parent, John, and I'm telling you to hold off. I want to talk to him first, and right now, he needs to heal."

I couldn't hear Dr. Erickson's response, but my mom must have prevailed as she walked in alone and said, "Let's go home."

****

On the ride home, the constant hum of the engine lulled me to sleep as it had when my dad used to drive me and Lindsey around the block several times, trying to get us to fall asleep when we were kids.

The sudden silence, then the creak of the car door, was an automatic wake-up call. My eyelids fluttered open to see my dad and Lindsey rushing out of our two-story house toward the car. Even with Brad's awesome suturing skills, a scowl cut into my dad's brow as he laid eyes on me, but Lindsey's face turned several shades of pale as she reached for our dad's hand, making my chin tremble.

"Mike, take Lindsey inside," Mom ordered, waving him away.

He ignored her, voicing his own demands. "Tell me what the hell happened!"

"I don't know what happened!" she fired back, raising her voice. "Just help me get him inside, but gently. His ribs are fractured."

"Jesus," he grumbled before hooking an arm underneath mine. "Diane, grab his other arm, and we'll help him to his room."

With my mom on one side and my dad on the other, I hobbled between them as they shuffled me inside and up to my bedroom, while Lindsey followed behind, the same terrified expression plastered on her face. They set me on the bed, then my mom reached inside her purse, retrieving the prescription. "Lindsey, go downstairs and get a glass of water for your brother, please."

Lindsey nodded, then raced out of the room. The patter of her feet jogging down the stairs echoed against the walls of my brain. I let out a groan, pressing my fingertips to my temples. My mom pulled my hands away. "No, honey, don't touch your face. I've got your pain meds right here as soon as Lindsey gets back with the water."

My dad met Lindsey at the door, took the water from her, and set the tall glass on my nightstand. He jammed his hands into his pockets, then shook his head. "This makes no sense. Brandon..."

Before he got a chance to finish, Mom barked out, "Not now, Mike!" Then handed me a pill and the water. I downed the pill with one gulp of water. "Lindsey, why don't you go help your dad with dinner. I'll be down after I get Brandon settled."

Lindsey nudged his arm. "C'mon, Dad, that's our cue to leave."

He stood motionless, rooted to the floor, unwilling to leave. Lindsey grabbed onto his arm and dragged him into the hallway before shutting my bedroom door.

"Let's get you out of those bloodstained clothes," Mom said, pulling a pair of pajamas from my dresser drawer. "Do you want me to stay with you until you fall asleep?"

"I'm not a kid anymore, Mom."

"You'll always be my baby." She kissed the top of my head. "I'm not going to press now, but I'll be back later, and you *will* tell me what happened." She turned off the light and left my room.

As the door settled into its frame, I closed my eyes and let the codeine take over, pushing *that* conversation furthest from my mind.

Sometime later, I woke to a dimly lit room, and Lindsey, sitting cross-legged at the end of my bed, staring at me.

"Creeper," I said, struggling to sit up.

She hopped off the bed and propped me up against the pillows. "You look like Frankenstein."

"Gee, thanks, Lins."

My sarcasm seemed to fly right over her head. "Spill, and I want details."

I shivered as the bathroom brawl flashed behind my eyes. "Got jumped at school."

Her eyes widened. "Kids beat you up? Why?"

Mom came into the room before I could answer, placing her hands on her hips and shaking her head. "Lindsey, I told you not to disturb your brother."

"But Mom," she protested, "I have to know what happened."

"It's late, and you have school tomorrow." She pointed at the door. "Out."

Lindsey spun off in a huff. "So not fair."

Mom blocked the doorway with an arm, then gave Lindsey a hug. "Good night, Lindsey."

"Good night, Mom." Lindsey glanced back at me. "Night, Brandon."

"Night, Lins."

Mom surveyed my room like she was taking inventory of my life, letting her gaze linger on each of my personal possessions. After several minutes, she turned and faced me.

"Brandon, tell me what happened."

My brain scrambled, searching for a way to avoid the inevitable. "I can't."

"Yes, you can."

"You'll hate me."

Her hand flew to her chest and fluttered over her heart. "Why on earth would you say such a thing? I love you. You're my son."

I studied her for some time before I replied. "I'll tell you, but you can't say anything until I'm finished. Promise?"

She sat next to me on the bed, taking my hand. "I promise."

I sucked in a breath of air, then slowly released it. "Some of my fr...some kids jumped me—beat me up."

"What? Why would they do that?"

"Mom, please. You promised."

"You're right. I'm sorry."

"Because of something I did." I looked away and whispered, "Sam was on her period, and I could smell the blood. I wanted to taste the blood. I *needed* to taste the blood."

My mom's posture stiffened as she clutched at her hands.

"Brandon, this is nonsense. Listen to what you're saying."

"It sounds...crazy and...gross, but you have to let me finish."

She didn't respond, just sat there, motionless, with a dazed look on her face.

"So, I kissed her, then bit her tongue, tasting her blood in my mouth."

My mom flinched, then shivered. She must be thinking, *my son's sick in the head.*

"That same feeling came over me the next morning when you touched me. I felt your blood pumping under your skin, and I heard your heartbeat pounding in my ears." In a shrill voice, I rattled off the rest in bits and pieces. "When I went back to school, the whole class turned blood red. Mrs. Clark dragged me to the nurse. They jumped me to punish me for what I did to Sam. I split Will's lip wide open, and the blood..." My eyes released a flood of tears, streaming down my face. "I-I wa-wanted it. I tasted it, but then I r-ran. I ran!" I latched onto her hands and cried, "I'm really scared. I don't know what's happening to me. I'm sick or worse. Help me, please!"

Her arms encircled me, and she rocked me back and forth, humming softly in my ear as if she hadn't heard a word I'd said, before releasing me.

"I have a confession to make," she said calmly. "I've never told this to anyone, not even your father." She sharpened her tone. "Promise me you'll keep this between us."

I locked my gaze with hers. "I promise."

As she tucked her dark blonde hair behind her ears, she let her shoulders slump forward. "I knew you'd be different. I didn't want to admit it, and after 16 years, I had thought maybe...but what you've done confirms it."

"Different? Different how?"

She stared straight ahead as she said, "I was in labor for 19 hours with you. I was so exhausted and on pain medication, but I know what I saw."

I blinked several times before shaking my head and blurting out, "Mom, you're freaking me out. What are you talking about?"

She looked at me before returning her focus to the wall on the opposite side of the room. "I saw a girl, no more than 19 or 20, standing in the corner of the delivery room, watching me. I'll never forget her. She had these beautiful, jewel-like, ocean-blue eyes."

The mention of ocean-blue eyes sparked some hidden memory deep inside me. The hospital nurse had eyes like that, but she'd confirmed we'd never met.

My mom continued revealing the past, speaking so softly, I had to strain to hear her. "Your father, my doctor, and his nurse let this perfect stranger linger in my room. I remember pointing and shouting at her to get out, but she just stood there, and no one lifted a finger to remove her. I wondered if I was hallucinating from the drugs and she was just a figment of my imagination. A contraction hit, then another, and they didn't stop. The girl rushed to my bedside and placed her hand over my stomach, whispering something like, "Your baby will fill the hole in my heart." I tried to push her away, but your father took my hand and told me it was okay. Then you came into the world..."

My mom couldn't stop there. Who was the girl? What happened next? I needed answers. "Mom?"

She didn't respond, not even with a twitch of her brow.

I raised my voice. "Mom!"

She blinked several times before she resumed her story. "I heard your first cry and was about to take you in my arms when..." She tilted her head from side to side. "When something I can only describe as a glowing mist, hovered over the girl, then completely encased her. She sobbed as it wrenched itself away from her and flew full force at you, rushing into your mouth, then disappeared inside of you."

A bark of laughter flew out of my mouth. "Rushed into my mouth? Did it infect me? Is that what's wrong with me?"

"Let me finish." She didn't wait for a reply. "The girl just vanished, as if she'd never been there. I thrashed about the bed, flailing my arms and shrieking, 'My baby! Give me my baby!' My doctor quickly handed you over to your father, who had a look of horror on his face. It was quite clear they thought I'd lost my mind, and I knew I had to pull it together. I forced every muscle to relax, and in a gentle tone, I expressed how sorry I was. That the exhaustion and emotion had taken its toll, and for a moment I panicked. Relief spread across their faces, and the tension in the room lifted. My doctor laid you in my arms, and as I stared into your tiny, beautiful face, I swore never to tell another soul what I'd seen. As the years passed, I allowed myself to forget." An expression of sorrow pulled at the corners of her mouth. "But it did change you."

I stared at her with my mouth hanging open. My mom needed to get a grip. No way could any of that be true. I'd never heard of mist entering people. I mean, maybe in some horror movie, but this wasn't a movie, this was my life! After taking several deep breaths, I found my voice. "Mist? Really, Mom? And why didn't anyone else see the girl or the mist? It had to have been the drugs."

She sighed, then shook her head. "I don't have an explanation, I'm sorry. I wish I had answers."

I blew out an impatient snort. *She wished she had answers*? "You must know something. Why did this girl seek you out? Had you seen her before? And what about this mist stuff? Why would it want to enter me, a baby? You can't expect me to accept any of this."

Her arms came around me, holding me close. "We'll figure it out, I promise you."

****

I laid there, wide awake, running my mom's freaky story repeatedly through my brain. How could mist enter someone? It wasn't a living organism. It couldn't make decisions. But had it infected me? Was it controlling me from the inside? Did the mist hunger after human blood? I just didn't see how any of it could be true. Things like that didn't happen in the real world, yet I couldn't shake the nagging feeling that I knew the girl. Maybe I was confusing her with Sam, the girl who awakened this bloodthirsty thing inside me. And why now? What changed? Was 16 the magic age? Had I unknowingly flipped some hidden switch, activating the mist or whatever it was? Was I its prisoner? There were just too many questions and no answers. I gritted my teeth and growled out a strained breath.

My groan sent a sharp twinge plowing into my side. I grabbed onto my ribs, feeling tender flesh rippling underneath my fingertips as I cried out. Remembering the codeine, I reached for the bottle on the nightstand. My hand fumbled around, finding only the lamp. My mom must have taken the bottle with her, so I had two choices: sit and wait for her to return or go find her. Another pang of pain struck, and I didn't hesitate to choose the latter as I wrapped an arm around my ribs and sat up. Pain coiled through my rib cage, deflating me like a balloon. As I gripped the sheets, I grunted out a scream, waiting for the burning sting to ease up. After a few quick breaths, I touched one foot to the ground, then the other before rising off the bed and bearing my weight. A clenching spasm threw me off-balance, but I didn't give up as I hobbled across the hall, inching toward the staircase. I took one stair at a time, leaning against the wall for support. By the time I reached the bottom stair, my pj's were soaked in sweat.

Muffled voices buzzed on the other side of the stair wall— my parents' voices. I crept a little closer, tilting my head, straining to hear. Sharp tones cut through the silence, and I didn't hesitate to follow the heated exchange, leading me all the way to the kitchen. I hid behind the pantry, then peeked around its side into the kitchen. My dad's arms were locked over his chest, and my mom stood rigid. The only thing that moved was her head as she firmly shook it back and forth.

"Absolutely not, Diane. Brandon *will* go back to school," Dad affirmed in his unyielding manner, then pointed out, "I called the school and spoke to the Vice Principal. He assured me that no fights were reported."

"Did you *look* at our son, Mike?" Mom spoke in a softer tone but determined, nonetheless. "Of course, there was a fight. Fear of getting in trouble is probably what stopped the other kids from coming forward, and I'll be damned if I let something like this happen again. It's our responsibility to protect him."

"Of course, I noticed the beating he suffered," he snapped. "It burns me up inside, but since it wasn't reported, the school won't investigate. Brandon needs to come forth and make the school aware to ensure this never happens again. Taking him out of school is completely unnecessary. Besides, they're teenagers. Whatever the fight was about, they'll get over it."

"And what if they don't? What if we send him back and something worse happens?" she fired back.

My dad groaned loudly. "Then we put him in a different school. Homeschooling is only going to isolate him."

"I'm right about homeschool. You just have to trust me on this one."

"Maybe if you were making sense, but he got into one fight. Teenage boys do stupid stuff. It's up to us to teach him that fighting's not the answer."

"It's more than a fight, Mike." Her voice seemed to fail as she murmured, "He's not like other kids."

"He's just like every other kid. You're overreacting."

"I am not! We can hire a tutor. It's that simple."

A loud huff came out of Dad. "Don't be ridiculous. You're only magnifying the issue. Locking him up is not the answer. He needs normalcy. He needs to be around other teenagers."

"Am I? Those kids could have ended his life today. Do you want to take that chance?"

"Damn it, Diane. You're trying my patience."

My mom's voice quivered. "I h-have to p-protect him. *We* have to protect him!"

My dad threw his hands in the air. "Protect him from what? He's not reckless or wild. He's a good kid, always has been. What happened is very concerning, but you're being irrational."

I couldn't take their bickering a moment longer and shuffled into the kitchen to confront them. "Can I tell you what I want?"

Dad gave me the hands on the hips gesture. "Brandon, it's not up to you to decide."

Mom ignored him and quickly swiped at her eyes, brushing away tears. "Of course, you can tell us."

"Diane," Dad barked. "Brandon—"

"Tell us," she said again, cutting him off and turning to me.

From my viewpoint, I'd become dangerous. I couldn't control my actions, so isolating myself seemed like a reasonable solution, at least for the time being. I glanced back and forth between them before giving my answer. "If I go back to school, any school, I can't promise this won't happen again. Mom's right, homeschool is safer."

A dazed expression claimed my dad's face as he said, "Why would you say that son?"

Before I could respond, my mom tucked an arm around me, guiding me out of the kitchen. "Brandon, you should be resting. Let me help you back to your room." She had that "don't say a word" look plastered on her face as she slyly cut a hand across her throat.

I got it; she wanted my dad left in the dark, but why not fill him in? Wouldn't that be easier if he knew what had happened at my birth and how it connected to my problem now?

And what if my dad knew something about that day, something that could help? Maybe he'd kept quiet too. A sharp stab of pain interrupted my thoughts, and I blurted out, "The pain's back. Came downstairs looking for you."

"I'll get the codeine." She ushered me toward the stairs. "First, let me get you back in bed."

My dad reached inside one of the cabinets over the sink and pulled out the bottle. "Got it right here."

We took the stairs one at a time, with my dad bringing up the rear, holding a tall glass of water. They both helped me get back into bed, then covered me with the blankets.

"Are you comfortable? Do you need me to add another pillow?" Mom asked.

"I'm good, thanks."

"Here, son," Dad said, handing me a codeine pill and the water.

My mom kissed the top of my head. "Your father and I need to finish our conversation, and you need to get some rest."

I grabbed her hand. "You should tell him." Her eyes doubled in size as she stared down at me.

"Tell who what?" Dad asked.

I completely ignored her silent warning as I rattled off, "Tell Dad what you saw. Tell him about the mist. Tell him I'm infected. Tell him about the blood."

He wiped a hand over his narrow mouth, then shook his head. "Brandon, what are you rambling on about?" He glanced at my mom. "Diane, maybe you're giving him too much codeine."

She took her eyes off me for a second to glance back at my dad. "I'll check with John tomorrow. Mike, can you please check on Lindsey? Make sure she's doing her homework and not on her cell phone. I'll get Brandon settled, then I'll meet you in our room."

He stood for a moment, his gaze darting between my mom and me. "I'll check on her. She's on the phone way too much." He kissed my mom's cheek. "See you in a few." He gave my hand a squeeze. "Good night, son."

"Good night."

My mom focused on the doorway, watching the empty space for several seconds before she turned to me. "I know you mean well, but your father won't understand," she whispered, shaking her head. "Everything's black and white to him. You can't tell him."

"Do *you* even understand, Mom?" I threw back at her.

She sat on the bed, resting her hands in her lap where they trembled. "No, I don't," she confessed. "I'm trying to make sense of it all."

Twisting the sheets between my hands, I swallowed hard, fearing my situation would only get worse.

CHAPTER 5

My dad gave in and agreed to homeschool—like he ever had a choice—but only for the rest of the school year. My mom whipped up a list of candidates, six to be exact, and as she interviewed them within the boundaries of our leather furnished living room, I sat on the sidelines, scrutinizing the tutors. Five out of the six she rejected. What she was looking for, I wasn't sure, but what I wanted and needed was an open-minded, off-the-cuff individual who wouldn't judge me or freak out if I freaked out.

The loud rap at the door announced the final candidate. I slouched farther into the chair, then glanced toward the entryway, positive my mom would reject this person too.

As my mom answered the door, she hesitated a few seconds before asking, "Are you Rick Miles?"

In an unhurried tone, a male voice answered, "Yes, Mrs. Cass, I am. Pleased to meet you."

"And you. Please, come in."

It sounded like bicycle wheels rubbing against the stone entryway as he entered. I leaned over the chair, trying to get a glimpse of the guy.

"This way," Mom said, coming into the living room.

He didn't walk in. He effortlessly maneuvered his wheelchair over the thick carpet and stopped just right of the sofa. I sat upright, transfixed on his jagged scar cutting through his hairline and traveling all the way down the right side of his face to the corner of his mouth. A mutilated right ear peeked through his blackish colored hair. "What happened to you?" I blurted out.

My mom gasped out loud. "Brandon!" She quickly faced him, placing her hand over her heart. "I'm so sorry. Please, forgive my son."

His dark brown eyes glimmered with laughter. "No apology needed." Extending his hand, he greeted me. "Rick Miles, pleased to meet you."

I took his hand, giving it a firm shake. "Brandon, nice to meet you too." I wasn't the best judge of age, but he couldn't have been more than 25. Even through his faded blue jeans, I could see how skinny his legs were, but his arms looked like the Incredible Hulk's. How did he end up in a wheelchair? Again,

I asked, "What happened?"

My mom heaved a sigh as she shook her head at me.

"It's okay, Mrs. Cass," he chuckled. "His question is only natural. I was in a motorcycle accident when I was 17. Being young and foolish, I wasn't wearing a helmet. A car ran a red light and hit me head-on. The accident severed my spine. They say I'm lucky to be alive." He patted the side of his chair. "And this wheelchair has become my best friend."

My mom plastered on her heartfelt expression as she laid her hand on his shoulder. "Rick, I'm terribly sorry."

"Don't be," he said, shrugging it off. "It's all good now."

"How do you get around? Does someone drive you everywhere?" Mom flashed a disapproving glare my way, but I ignored her. I needed info.

He offered up the same chuckle before saying, "Nope. I drive myself. Got a van with all the bells and whistles for a guy in a wheelchair."

It came to me in a big bright flash inside my brain. *Pick this guy as your tutor*! I squished my brows together as I stared at him. His imperfection was visible and mine was not, but we both had them. I couldn't put my finger on the reason why, but I sensed he'd get me, that my unique set of circumstances wouldn't freak him out. I didn't hesitate to go with my gut. "I want you to be my tutor."

My mom barked out a laugh as her head jerked in my direction. "Brandon, Rick and I haven't had a chance to discuss his experience."

"I don't care." I paused, then glanced at Rick. His raised brow look suggested I'd caught him off guard too, but it had to be him. "Mom, please," I begged.

Her expression softened. "Give me a few minutes to look over his résumé." She didn't wait for a reply as she skimmed over the sheet of paper. After several long minutes, she turned to Rick. "The agency wasn't kidding. My goodness, you have quite an impressive résumé."

His lips spread into a wide grin. "Why, thank you. I believe there's nothing more important than education. I take it very seriously." He reached into his briefcase and handed her more sheets of paper. "I also brought several letters of recommendation."

My mom engrossed herself in his letters, like reading a gripping novel. She finally met his eyes. "Rick, I couldn't be happier. The position is yours, if you want it."

My stomach clenched, and I held my breath, awaiting his reply. He narrowed his gaze at me. Maybe he sensed something off about me or wondered the reason behind the home-schooling, but whatever deterred him vanished, and he jetted out his hand. "I accept."

I exhaled and gave a thumbs-up.

My mom gestured in my direction and pointed out the elephant in the room. "Brandon's recovering from an accident. Can you start in two weeks?"

"Two weeks it is."

CHAPTER 6

Rick's arrival came with an abundance of rain. The murky, gray sky growled, dumping pails of hail. The icy pellets flew in every direction, hammering our entryway and Rick. My mom held the door wide open as she hurriedly waved him inside. "Come inside and out of this nasty weather."

He shook out his umbrella before entering. "Thank you, Mrs. Cass. Man, mother nature decided to give us a piece of her mind today."

"Yes, she sure did," she agreed, pushing the door closed and shutting out the cold. "I've got hot coffee brewing in the kitchen. Would you like a cup?"

"That would be fantastic. Thank you."

My mom gave him one of her pleasant smiles, then glanced my way. "Brandon, please show Rick to the den."

I pointed toward the hallway. "It's down that hallway, second door on the right. Do you need help?"

"I got it, thanks," he said, giving the wheels a spin as he veered toward the hall.

I hurried in front of him, making sure the door stood wide open. "In here," I said, letting him enter.

A toasty blanket of heat rolled forward from the fireplace, welcoming us. He passed the wall of built-ins stacked with books and parked his wheelchair next to my dad's oversized recliner. I plopped down on the L-shaped sectional, opposite him. His heartbeat thumped at a relaxed, normal rhythm, though he had no idea what he'd walked in to, and I had no idea when another blood craving would hit. Hopefully, it wouldn't happen in front of him.

Rick tapped the corner of his brow. "You got your stitches out."

"Yeah, a couple days ago. My doctor says I won't have any scars." I cringed and inwardly shrank. What a complete idiot. I held out my hand in an apologetic gesture. "Rick, I'm sorry. That came out all wrong."

He shrugged and offered up a bemused grin. "No worries, man. It's a strange world we live in. If you don't fit the mold, then you weren't meant to be."

"Yeah…" Should I elaborate? I decided to go for it. "There's something you should know about me. I mean, why I'm not in school."

"No need to explain. I know where you're coming from. I don't judge. God is the only judge in my world."

God? What did I know about God? My mom came through the door, carrying a steaming cup of coffee and a tray of pastries, saving me from attempting a response.

"Thank you, Mrs. Cass." Rick held the mug under his nose and took a good whiff. "Smells delicious."

"You're welcome. I'll leave you two to your lesson." She stopped in the doorway. "Oh yes, I wanted to ask what time you think you'll break for lunch, Rick?"

"Usually around noon," he answered.

She nodded. "I'll be back then with some sandwiches. Sound good?"

He gave a firm nod. "Sounds great."

"All right then." She closed the door, leaving us alone.

I ran my hand through my hair. "How long did it take you to grow your hair out?"

"Years." He opened his briefcase and began to rummage through it. His bicep muscle flexed as he retrieved a reference book, a legal pad, and a pencil.

"How long have you been working out?"

Rick looked up at me and again said, "Years. What's your least favorite subject in school?"

I groaned out the word like it was a disease. "His-tor-y."

"Then let's get it out of the way," he insisted, handing me a history book. "Read chapters one through three."

I snatched the book away from him. "Nice fake-out."

"They're short chapters. It won't take long."

I heaved a sigh, propped the book onto my knees and flipped to chapter one. Five pages in, I lost focus on the boring exploration and colonization of America and glanced over at Rick. As he scribbled frantically across the page of some type of journal spread open in his lap, his face grew flushed and moist with perspiration. With each stroke of his pen, the hurried thud of his heart vibrated inside my ears. He seemed on edge, and something had spiked his heartbeat. I had to know what. I left the couch and stepped toward him. "Are you okay?"

He snapped the journal closed, then centered on me, still gripping the pen. "What?" He struggled to smile. "Nothing. Keep reading."

"No, something's wrong. What is it?"

He stared at the floor as he let out a low sigh. "I keep this journal, recording my thoughts about life. It's my way of letting everything out. Sometimes, I get frustrated. I know I said I had it under control, but really, it's a work in progress."

This was my opportunity to share as well. "I get it. On the outside, I look totally normal, but what you can't see is what's on the inside. I don't know how or why, but something changed me. It's hard for me to be around people." I looked down at the floor. "I've hurt people."

A deep frown creased his brow. "What do you mean, hurt people?"

The sudden shattering of glass, then my sister's high-pitched squeal shelved my response. She shouldn't be home. Was something wrong? I dashed out of the den and sprinted in the direction of her cries, the whirl of Rick's wheelchair following close behind. Her screams morphed into one continuous howl with no breaths in between. The pitch lifted the hair off the back of my neck and aimed me toward the kitchen. I darted around the island, then trampled into a pool of brilliant red staining the polished slate tiles before screeching to a halt.

Mom was at the sink, grabbing a towel. Her eyes bulged from their sockets as they met mine. "Brandon, look away," she warned. "Don't come in."

Her words of caution came too late. The sparkling chunk of glass embedded in my sister's blood-gushing foot had already monopolized every cell inside my brain. Lindsey showered the floor with even more blood by her frantic jumping up and down. The thick, rich, coppery scent rushed up my nostrils, awaking an incredible hunger and beckoning me to come have a taste.

The memory of Lindsey vanished, and a blood sacrifice formed before me. Saliva spilled out the corners of my mouth and rolled down my chin. As I squeezed my fingers around the flesh oozing with blood, I trembled, barely able to breathe. High-pitched shrieks struck my eardrums. I didn't lose focus; the blood commanded me—nothing else mattered.

Hands gripped the base of my neck, yanking me backward and pushing me to the floor, freeing my prey. The bloody form scurried out of sight. I growled in rage and clenched my fists, then a speck of red glistened to my right. I inched forward on my hands and knees, following the droplets until I came upon a tasty treasure of bright red blood spreading across the slate tile. I flattened my body against the floor and darted out my tongue, devouring every inch of the sticky red serum. As the last drop slid down my throat, I shivered, craving more. My gaze skimmed each tile, hoping to spot a flicker of red, but what I found was Rick's bug-eyed, gaping mouth expression. I knew that look—Sam had it, and so did Will—fear! The dazed fog congesting my brain started to clear. Why was I on the floor? And why was I covered in blood? Oh God, I'd done it again, but to who? I cradled my throbbing head in my hands and rocked back and forth, thinking, *I'm going to be sick.*

Hurried footsteps came up from behind, and my mom's voice cut through the silence. "Rick, Rick." Then she shouted, "Rick!"

He slowly inched his head toward her.

She didn't give him a chance to speak as she blurted out, "I don't have time to explain. Lindsey needs a doctor. I have no right to ask this of you, and I wouldn't blame you if you turned and ran for the hills, but I'm a mother and both my kids need help. Please stay with Brandon until I get back. It's not his fault." Her voice weakened. "I'm sorry. I'm so sorry."

"I'll..." He hesitated a good while. "Yes, I'll stay."

"Thank you," she whispered, then I heard the pounding of her feet rushing out of the room.

The immediate thud of the door as it shut left Rick and I alone. I kept my gaze lowered as I asked, "Did I hurt Lindsey?"

Rick came out with a high-pitched, "Jesus, man, you tried to suck the blood from your sister's foot!" The urgency in his voice eased off as he added, "But licking the blood off the floor was the freakiest thing I've ever seen."

As tears streamed down my face, I screamed, "But did I hurt Lindsey!?" I jerked my head toward him. "Why am I covered in blood?"

"No, you didn't," he said in a calm, steady voice. "She cut her foot on some glass. You're covered in it because you laid in it."

A gush of relief blasted past my lips, but the sobs refused to let go. "I'd never forgive myself if I hurt her. S-she's m-my sister!" I bawled.

He squeezed my shoulder. "Calm down. Take a breath and try to relax. Your mom took her to the doctor. She'll be okay."

"I didn't hurt her. I didn't hurt her," I mumbled into my hands, rocking back and forth.

"Now might be a good time to finish that conversation we started before your sister screamed. You were going to tell me about why you've hurt people."

I threw my hands in the air and shouted, "You saw with your own eyes! What more is there to say?"

He looked me dead in the eyes and stated, "She cut her foot on glass. You had nothing to with that. What you did afterward, you're responsible for." He paused as his gaze traveled the length of the room, then returned to me. "You're covered in blood. You should change, and then we can talk."

I bobbed my head in agreement and pushed to my feet.

"First, I gotta wipe up the floor, make sure it doesn't stain."

He arched his brow. "Are you sure? Can't that wait?"

I stared at the hint of red coating the floor, then inhaled a deep breath. No cravings hit. "I gotta do it now." I grabbed a bottle of floor cleaner from underneath the sink and a handful of paper towels and scrubbed each tile, mumbling, "I'm a freak."

"I didn't say *you're* a freak. I said it was the freakiest thing I'd ever seen."

"What's the difference?"

"There's a significant difference."

"I guess." I tossed the soiled towels into the garbage with a little more force than necessary. "I'm gonna go upstairs and change. I'll meet you back in the den."

Rick nodded, then headed down the hall as I ran up the stairs. In my bathroom, I shed my clothes, washed the blood off, and threw on a clean pair of jeans and a T-shirt. I glanced at my bloodstained clothes lying on the floor. *They should go in the trash too.* I scooped them up, running as fast as I could to the garbage bin outside and pitched them inside. Hot tears burned behind my eyelids. I swiped them away, refusing to let the pain in. I would *not* become this monster! My chest rose and fell as my breaths came quicker and quicker, until I clenched my fists and belted out a scream. I slammed the bin closed and ran back into the house. As I trudged down the hall toward the den, I tried to shake off the unease to regain my composure before I faced Rick.

In the doorway, my shoulders stooped forward as I heaved a sigh. Was I prepared to tell a stranger what I'd done? Probably not, but what choice did I have? After what he'd seen, he deserved an explanation. I entered the den and paced the room as I unfolded my story. "Okay, first, I just want to say that for 16 years, I was normal. Never hurt any-one. Never had horrible thoughts. Never acted out. About a month ago, everything changed." I paused, gauging Rick's reaction. His straight-faced expression and peaceful heart-beat told me I could continue. "It started with this girl, Sam. I...I hurt her, made her bleed on purpose." In the center of the room, I came to a standstill, then sank into the couch. "I think there's something inside me that has a thirst for blood and picks up on heartbeats."

A dazed look spread over Rick's face. "That statement needs a little more clarification. What do you mean, *something* inside you?"

"I wish I could explain it, but that's just it, I can't."

He didn't respond, just continued to stare at me with that dazed look.

I frowned back at him, then let it go. He had every right to express shock, and I hadn't even gotten to my mom's crazy part of the story. "My parents took me out of school because I got the crap beat out of me for what I did to Sam, but what they don't know is that I fought back, and again, the urge to taste blood came over me. I did taste it, but then I ran."

Rick glided his hand over his mouth. "Maybe it's some sort of illness."

I sighed. "Been there, done that. My doctor says there's nothing wrong with me, and it gets worse."

He blinked, then narrowed his gaze. "Worse? How so?"

"My mom..." I cleared my throat. "She told me that on the day I was born, this girl and some sort of mist came after me."

His mouth hung slack as the dazed look gave way to a wide-eyed gaze. "Mist! How is that even possible?"

I bounced my foot against the floor and shook my head. "She says it entered me."

A bark of laughter rushed out of his mouth. "Brandon, that sounds, well..."

"Crazy," I answered for him. "I know, but she swears it happened."

He sat back in his wheelchair and tapped his fingers together, as if pondering the idea. "Interesting."

"Interesting?" Was he as demented as my mom?

"Definitely not the word I'd use."

He looked me directly in the eyes as he said, "I think I may know someone who can shed some light on this. Eve, a friend of mine, and a psychic."

I jiggled my earlobe as if I hadn't heard him right. "You can't be serious."

"She's authentic," he argued. "Her psychic abilities are mind-boggling, and she could possibly tell you what really happened at your birth."

Before I could voice my opinion, my mom walked in on us. I sprang off the couch, babbling out, "Where's Lindsey? What happened? Is she okay?"

My mom wrapped her arm around me and gave me a reassuring squeeze. "She's in her room, resting, and she's fine."

"I have to see her," I insisted, pushing past her.

I bolted up the stairs and skidded to a stop in front of Lindsey's bedroom door, which stood ajar. I could see her on her bed, holding a pillow and staring out the window. A pair of crutches stood propped against the wall by her bed. I didn't dare enter her purple palace after what I'd done, so I gently gave the door a push, then knocked. Her gaze darted to the open doorway, then grew cold and unforgiving as it fell on me. "Get out!" she shouted.

"Lins, please," I begged, feeling the weight of sobs choking me. "I want...*need* to apologize."

She chucked the pillow at me. "I said, get out!"

I stood in the doorway, trembling. "I would never hurt you."

She jutted a finger at me. "What do you call sucking blood from my foot then?"

The sting of her words made me flinch. My breath hitched. The tears came, falling in droves. I did nothing to hide them. "I didn't know what I was doing. There's something wrong with me."

"I'll say."

I sank against the frame, pressing my forehead to the door. "I don't know what's happening to me, and I'm really scared. Please, forgive me."

The hateful glare faded and her features softened. "Scared? What are you talking about?"

"Um, well, I..."

She waved me forward. "You can come in."

A gush of relief flew out of my mouth. "Thank you." I sat on the end of her bed and threw everything at her. "Mom says I'm different, altered at birth by mist. It changed me. I crave blood and hear heartbeats. I'm not normal."

Her face grew pale as her eyes doubled in size. "What? Why would Mom say that? And it doesn't even make sense."

My chin started to quiver as I blurted out, "I bit Sam."

She grabbed onto my arm. "You bit Sam? Crushing all over you, Sam? Brandon, why? Why would you do that?" Sobs mounted inside my throat, fighting to get out.

"Because I'm a freak," I cried.

"My brother is *not* a freak."

"I don't want to be this way. I don't want to hurt people. I'm afraid. What if I do something..."

Her arms came around me, pulling me close. "You won't. I won't let you. We have each other's backs, remember?"

I fell into her embrace, blubbering to the point where I couldn't utter a single word.

She hugged me tight as she whispered, "It's okay. Don't cry."

"Brandon?" Mom's voice filtered through my sobs. "We're going to figure this out, I promise."

"How?" I challenged. "No one knows what's happening."

I pointed at her and accused, "You're even afraid to tell Dad."

"Mom, what's going on?" Lindsey demanded.

Mom sat between us, wrapping an arm around each of us. "I have no idea."

"That's not acceptable," Lindsey fired back.

"Maybe we should go back to see Dr. Stewart?" Mom offered up.

I popped off the bed and adamantly shook my head. "This is beyond Dr. Stewart. We need answers about my birth. Rick says his psychic friend might be able to help."

A wide grin spread across Lindsey's face. "A psychic! Ooh, I'm in."

Mom raised her brow. "Rick filled me in on his friend, Eve. I wasn't at all thrilled you decided it was okay to discuss our private matters with someone we've only just met."

"Mom, come on, I had to say something. He saw what I did."

She heaved a sigh. "I know I'm going to regret this, but I'm desperate. I left Rick in the den on the phone with Eve."

I hugged my mom and whispered, "Thank you." For the first time since this whole mess started, a sense of calm washed over me. Maybe this Eve person could truly shed some light on my curse, disease, or whatever was plaguing me.

The squeak of the front door drifted up the staircase and into Lindsey's room. "Hey all, I'm home," Dad called out.

Mom pressed a finger to her lips. "Not a word of this to your father. I need to get a handle on this first."

"I think we should tell him," I said.

Lindsey busted out laughing. "No way. Dad's too uptight. He'll just freak. Mom's right."

"Where is everyone?" Dad called out a little louder.

"I need to go introduce your father to Rick," Mom said, then wiggled a finger at Lindsey and me. "As far as the two of you are concerned, Lindsey cut her foot and I took her to the doctor, nothing more." She gave a crisp nod and left the room.

I glanced at Lindsey, then scrunched my brows together.

"Why were you home anyway?"

She huffed. "Left my English essay on my nightstand. I ditched class to come home and was sneaking barefoot through the side door when I scared the crap out of Mom. She jumped, I jumped, and we knocked over the giant butterfly vase. My foot landed on a chunk of glass."

I smirked. "Nice one, Lins."

She punched my shoulder. "Shut up and help me with my crutches."

I placed a crutch under each arm. "Okay, but hurry up. We need to save Rick from Dad's third degree."

"I can't take the stairs alone. You have to help me."

"Fine." I held onto her arm as she hobbled down each step, one at a time.

At the middle stair, Mom's hostess-like tone met my ears.

"Mike, this is Rick Miles. Rick, this is my husband, Mike."

I heard Rick respond with, "Nice to meet you, Mr. Cass."

Dad sounded off one of his fake laughs before saying,

"And you. Now, call me Mike. So how did the first day go?"

Rick's reply was brief. "Very well."

"Homeschooling is new to us, and I have my reservations about the entire process. Do you mind if I ask you some questions?"

"Sure thing, Mr. Cass. I welcome questions from the parents."

"Call me Mike."

Rick barked out a quick laugh. "Sorry, just a habit."

I leaned over and whispered in Lindsey's ear, "Why isn't Mom saying something? Let me just pick you up so we can interrupt Dad before he lays into Rick."

"Chill. We're almost there, and I have a plan that will stop Dad cold."

Dad fired off his first question. "How long have you been tutoring?"

"Straight out of college. Three years."

"And how many students are you currently tutoring?"

"Other than Brandon, I have two full-time students. I also run an afterschool program and work with a group of 15 students with learning disabilities."

"Well, I commend you for that. What about your credentials? Can you tell me about your background?"

"Mike, this isn't necessary," Mom finally objected. "I've already reviewed Rick's experience."

"I'm sure Rick..." Dad began, then trailed off as his gaze fell on Lindsey and her crutches. He pulled his unruly brows together, then hooked an arm around her and kissed the top of her head. "What on earth happened?"

Lindsey winked at me. I guess this was part of her plan.

Mom shrugged. "I broke a vase."

"And I stepped on it," Lindsey chimed in.

Dad gave Lindsey another squeeze. "I'm so sorry, sweetheart. What can I do?"

She looked up at him with big eyes and said, "Ben and Jerry's Chocolate Chip Cookie Dough?"

"You got it." He turned to Rick and shook his hand. "Rick,

I'm sorry, I've gotta run and get my baby girl some ice cream."

Rick chuckled. "I totally understand."

My dad kissed my mom on the cheek. "I'll be back in 10." Then he headed out the door.

A proud grin spread across Lindsey's face as she nudged my side. "Told ya I had a plan."

I acknowledged her with a brief nod. I was much more interested in finding out about Eve. "So, what did Eve say?"

"She's very interested in meeting you," Rick divulged.

"Eve thrives on this kind of stuff."

I shot my arms overhead into a V. "Awesome."

"And she's agreed to meet us?" Mom asked.

"Yes, at 11 a.m. tomorrow," Rick confirmed, then pushed his hands in a downward fashion. "But whether she'll learn anything or not, that is yet to be seen."

Lindsey's eyes sparkled. "I am so there."

"Absolutely not," Mom sounded off in a stern voice. "You'll stay home and off that foot. Doctor's orders and mine."

"Mom, c'mon. It's not like we'll be walking around."

I shrugged my shoulders and offered up, "I kinda want Lins there."

"You two tag teaming me isn't going to change my answer. It's still no."

Lindsey groaned. "Fine. Whatever."

Mom ignored Lindsey's griping and centered her attention on Rick. "Rick, I'd appreciate it if you keep this matter between us."

"Of course. Oh, and Eve asked that you bring a personal item with you, something that you kept from that day, like a piece of jewelry or a memento of sorts."

"I was wearing my grandmother's locket."

"That's perfect."

"I'll make sure to bring it with me. Now, if you'll excuse me, I need to get dinner started. Rick, would you like to stay?"

Rick gave my mom a warm smile. "No thanks, Mrs. Cass. In fact, I need to get going. I have to meet my workout partner at six. Well, good night. See everyone in the morning."

From the living room window, I watched Rick's van vanish down the street and into the darkness. I finally had a smidgen of hope, but this person named Eve could take it all away with a single word. Would she provide answers or create only questions? Tomorrow seemed so far away.

CHAPTER 7

Rick rang the doorbell on the off-white cottage with the bright red door, then glanced back at my mom. "Your first time with a psychic?"

"Yes," Mom said, staring up at the wind chimes dangling from the porch and jingling in the breeze.

"Don't worry, Eve's harmless," Rick chuckled.

I didn't care who Eve was. I only cared about answers and getting my life back. The door opened, and a girl with cherry red lips stepped out onto the porch. Her short, jet-black hair framed her snow-white skin, and my brain conjured up the image of a mime.

She bent down and kissed Rick's cheek. "Hello, Rick."

Rick gave her a quick hug, then gestured to us. "Eve, this is Mrs. Cass and her son, Brandon. Mrs. Cass, Brandon, meet Eve."

She looked as though she'd just stepped out of the past, clothed in a tie-dyed halter top and bell-bottom jeans. She stuck out her pale hand. "Nice to meet you both."

My mom shook her hand. "And you."

Eve's brown eyes locked onto mine, staring intensely. She let the silence build before she spoke. "Hello, Brandon."

"Hi."

She waved us forward. "Please, come inside." A mixture of neutral colors and fabrics decorated her front room, completely opposite of the dramatic Eve. "Let me show you to my reading room." She led us down a hallway toward an open door.

My gaze traveled over the mahogany-colored walls, ornate beads curtaining the windows, lava lamps illuminating the room, and four large bean bag chairs surrounding a circular wooden table. The room was a prefect replica of Eve.

"Please, take a seat," she said, gesturing toward the bean bag chairs.

My mom lowered herself onto one of the chairs and pulled me down next to her. She took the locket from her purse and placed it in her lap. "We're hoping you can shed some light on what's happening to my son."

Rick claimed a spot in the back of the room, while Eve sat on the opposite side of me and my mom. She placed a white cloth over the table, then reached into a glass jar filled with clear liquid and needles. "I will reveal everything that is shown to me. Hopefully, it will help."

The two needles Eve pulled from the jar made me swallow hard. What the hell were those for?

Eve's eyes darted back and forth between me and my mom. "I must spill a drop of your blood onto this cloth, and it will tell me of your past, present, and future."

My mom shot Rick a look, then leveled her gaze on Eve. "Blood? I've never heard of such a thing. What kind of psychic are you?"

Eve's cherry red lips curved into a flashy grin. "I'm a medium and also a Wiccan."

"What's a Wiccan?" I asked.

"It's a witch," Mom answered, then grabbed my arm and yanked me to my feet. "We're done here."

A witch? I hadn't even wrapped my head around the whole psychic thing.

Rick jerked his wheelchair an inch or two closer to my mom. "Mrs. Cass, wait. I'm sure you're not pleased that I left that piece out, but I thought Eve should be the one to tell you."

"And you'd be right, Rick," Mom fired back.

Eve tossed a heated brow at Rick. "I agree. He should have informed you, but you're already here. I promise you, I will reveal the information you seek."

"This is outside my comfort zone," Mom expressed. "I can't—"

I cut her off. "If a few drops of blood are all she needs to get to the truth, then I'll give them." I centered my gaze on Eve. "I have to warn you, though, blood affects me, and not in a safe way. I might not be able to control myself."

Eve didn't seem the slightest bit concerned as she said, "I can form a barrier around the blood so the only one it impacts is me."

"Please, Mom, I want to do this."

"I don't like it," Mom huffed, shaking her head.

"I assure you, my methods are very safe. You and Brandon will not be harmed in any way."

My mom looked at me with an expression of hope, then turned to Eve. "As you stated, we're already here, but if anything seems off, I'll stop it at once and take Brandon out of here."

"Of course," Eve agreed. "Now, did you bring the item I asked for?"

"Yes." Mom handed over her locket.

Eve barely glanced at the locket before placing it in the center of the table. She picked up one of the needles and reached for my hand. "Let's get started."

Eve pricked my finger, then squeezed out a large drop of blood. As I rubbed away the sting, I watched a perfect round dot of red form on the fabric. I sat still, with every muscle straining against my skin, waiting for the bloodthirsty monster inside me to take over. Seconds flew by without an urge, crazy thought, or incredible hunger. Limb by limb, I relaxed, then sank in my seat.

My mom wrinkled her brow, then rested her hand on my forearm. "Brandon, are you alright?"

"I'm good."

"Mrs. Cass, your hand," Eve requested in an insistent tone.

My mom's gaze lingered on me for a long while before she finally offered her hand. Eve dropped my mom's blood onto the cloth next to mine, then held her hands directly over our scarlet imprints and chanted in some language I'd never heard. Her forehead twisted as if she were in pain, then relaxed. Eve closed her eyes and fell silent. She sat that way for several minutes before her eyes fluttered open and she began to speak. "The origin of this blood links to a handful of beings. It is ancient, powerful, unearthly...a male...a female. It is also youthful, vulnerable, mortal...a mother...a son." She swayed her head back and forth. "This blood was given and received to save a life...a mother's life."

I compressed my lips while Eve rattled on, having no clue what she was talking about. Though the way my mom clenched and unclenched her jaw, and the fierce storm raging inside her eyes, told me the words meant something to her. Had Eve struck a nerve, gotten too close to the truth, dredged up something my mom wanted to forget?

Eve snatched up the locket, closing it inside the palm of her hand, then extended her free one toward me. "We must join hands, Brandon."

As Eve laced our fingers, a hazy film brushed over the color of her eyes. "I sense the essence of a young but powerful female around this locket. The entity planted inside you connects to her. Its energy is not hurtful nor evil. I feel an aura of love and hope. It will not harm you, but you may harm others because of it. This entity covets the young woman and yearns to reunite with her. It will pursue her at all costs. You must allow the power inside you to lead you to the answers you seek." She blinked, then her eyes cleared. "That is all I see."

I squeezed her hand hard. "What? No! There must be more. I don't know what any of that means. What entity? What girl? Please, tell me!"

She released my hand and handed the locket to my mom. "Brandon." She said my name in a calm, soft voice. "I have revealed all that was exposed to me. The power will guide you. Don't fight it. It will reveal the answers you seek."

My mom shoved the locket in her purse, then quickly got to her feet, pulling me with her. "I've heard enough. We're leaving."

"Mom, wait," I protested, stretching around to face Eve. "Please, is there anything else? Even if it's the tiniest thing. Please!"

Eve shook her head. "I'm sorry, that is all I know." Eve took my mom's hands and said, "I understand your reservation to believe, but please know I meant no harm and only tried to help."

"That goes for me too, Mrs. Cass," Rick offered up.

My mom acknowledged them with a slight nod before saying, "I believe you both acted with the best of intentions, but I have to handle this matter the way I see fit, and that way doesn't involve entities and sharing of souls."

Eve's lips spread into a bemused smile. "I understand."

"Of course," Rick answered.

My mom's hang-ups weren't mine. I planned to dive deeper and learn as much as I could, even if it was behind her back.

****

After dinner that evening, I helped my mom load the dishwasher for the sole purpose of bringing up the session with Eve. I desperately needed to know if what was said meant anything to her, and she'd been very tight-lipped about the whole thing. "Are we gonna talk about this?"

My mom's hands were full of silverware when she turned to me. "Brandon..." She suddenly cried out and dropped everything on the floor, then cradled a finger, dripping with blood. "Damn it!"

The salty, rich scent rushed up my nostrils, sending my heart into a beating frenzy and saliva flooding over my tongue. I stepped closer, possessed by the blood.

"No, Brandon, stop!" The sharp tone of her voice pierced my brain.

I turned away and held my breath. Using every ounce of strength within me, I fled the kitchen and the blood I craved, racing out of the house and into the garage. Energy pulsed through my veins, bad energy, energy I needed to release. My hands trembled as I skimmed the garage, searching. My dad's bench press caught my attention. I loaded weights on either side, slid underneath, and pounded out 20 presses. The power inside weakened, and I became me again. Was lifting weights a way to control the power? It wasn't a cure, but until I found a better solution, it was a temporary fix to rid myself of the entity.

The side door opened, and my mom called out, "Brandon, are you in here?"

"Here, Mom. Lifting weights."

She entered the garage with her hands behind her back. A half-smile came to her face. "You fought it. That's a great sign."

I sat up and shrugged. "Yeah."

She sat next to me and handed me a small envelope. "Your birthday's a little more than a week away, but under the circumstances, I thought you deserved something to cheer you up and get your mind off things."

I ripped it open. "A gift card to Music World! Cool." I gave her a kiss on the cheek. "Thanks, Mom."

She stroked my hair and smiled at me. "You're welcome. Hey, I need to pick up a few things at the grocery store. Want to tag along? I can drop you off at Music World while I shop.

We've still got plenty of time before they close."

I gave her a high-five. "I'm in."

"Great. Let me just tell your father and get my purse."

I jumped off the bench and waited by the car. We were on the road in less than five minutes, heading to Westhaven Mall. It seemed like the perfect time to bring up Eve. I twisted in my seat to face my mom. "Are we ever going to talk about what happened at Eve's?"

She took her eyes off the road for a brief second. "She said a lot of bizarre things. Honestly, Brandon, I have no idea what any of it meant, and I don't want to know, nor should you."

My mom was crazy if she thought I'd just let it go. "Mom, c'mon. I mean, it was so out there that it had to be true. She couldn't have made it up, right?"

She let out a huff. "Ancient, unearthly blood; powerful entities; soul sharing? It sounds absurd."

"And what I've done doesn't?"

She reached over and smoothed my hair. "We're going to get through this, I promise."

I humored her with a smile and a nod, but I took Eve's words to heart. Knowing what to do with them or how to let the power lead me was another story.

The car slowed as my mom turned into the mall's parking lot. She pulled up in front of Music World and let the engine idle. "I'll probably be about a half hour or so. Don't wait for me in the parking lot. Wait inside the store."

I rolled my eyes. "Mom, the grocery store is three stores down." Before she could object, I held up my hands and added, "But I'll wait inside, I promise."

She gave me a squeeze. "Thank you. See you in a few."

"See ya." I watched the car vanish around the corner before shoving the gift card into my pocket and setting out to claim my prize. The doors of Music World slid wide open, and I trekked inside. The place reminded me of Disneyland, with everyone zigzagging up and down the aisles as if waiting to jump on their favorite ride, but in this case, grab their CD of choice. I was no different as I roamed through the store, skimming CD titles and occasionally flipping one over to read the back.

In less than 15 minutes, I'd cherry-picked The Chainsmokers, Twenty One Pilots, Maroon 5, and Fall Out Boy. With the $100 gift card, I had enough for one more and continued scanning the row of CDs. I'd gotten halfway up the aisle when a girl with chocolate-brown hair passed me, her long hair swaying back and forth down her back, and a velvety soft strand brushed against my bare arm. Electricity surged through me, jolting my heart. I clutched at my shirt and let out a gasp. She stopped inches away, and the scent of lavender and vanilla perfumed the air, spinning my head. She flipped through a cluster of CDs, shook her head, and continued down the aisle as if I weren't even there. I knew her, this beautiful creature, and I couldn't lose her again. I bolted after her and shouted, "Hypatia, wait."

She rounded the corner of the row without so much as a glance in my direction.

I caught up to her and latched onto her arm, forcing her to stop. Again, I said the name I knew. "Hypatia."

She yanked her arm free and shoved me away with both hands. "What the hell, dude?"

A pair of solid brown orbs glared at me. I blinked, rubbed my eyes, and blinked again. Who was this girl? I had no idea. Why had I stopped her? Why had I called her Hypatia? I backed away, holding up my hands in a surrendering gesture. "I'm so sorry. I thought you were someone else."

"Whatever," she huffed, dismissing me as she stomped off.

I scratched my head as I stared at where she'd stood. *Who the hell was Hypatia?* I replayed the scene in my head; the girl's hair triggered some distant memory, like the nurse at the hospital. "Hypatia," I said the name out loud, and my skin grew fiery hot. For some strange reason, I started humming that lullaby I'd heard as a kid. It led me to the New Age section where I combed through the CDs, examining the titles until I plucked one from its slot. I marched over to the register with complete confidence, laid the CDs on the counter, and handed over my gift card.

CHAPTER 8

Alone in my bedroom, I ripped open the New Age CD and popped it into the player. As a mixture of piano, harp, and guitar danced inside my head, a sense of peace washed over me. My eyelids grew heavy and my body sluggish. I staggered over to my bed and fell on top of the mattress, then scooped my arms underneath my pillow and drifted off to sleep.

A beautiful girl broke through the surface of my dream. Her flowing, chocolate-brown hair and ocean-blue eyes were ones I'd seen thousands of times before. She drew near, reaching for me with open arms. My heart drummed against my chest, beating faster and faster as I rushed toward her, just as she vanished into the darkness. I spun around in every direction, yelling out one name—Hypatia. My grumbled screaming snapped me awake, and my eyes flew wide open as I sat straight up. Her image haunted my mind. Was it a dream? For a brief second, I hoped it wasn't and skimmed over my room, then my heart sank, finding no one. Who was this girl I kept seeing in people? First the nurse, then the girl at the music store, and now inside my dream. Awareness trickled down the skin of my arms. I knew because I'd called out her name—Hypatia. A soft tap at my door interrupted my concentration. "Come in."

The door cracked, and my mom peeked in. "Just wanted to check in on you before I went to bed." She paused and stood still, then tilted her head. "This music is lovely. When did you start liking this kind of music?"

I shrugged. "Today, I guess."

She laughed. "Today?"

"I think the thing inside me likes this music."

She crossed her arms in a huff. "The thing inside you! Brandon, don't let Eve's words influence you."

"This has nothing to do with Eve." My gaze traveled away from her and focused on the ceiling. "This is about Hypatia."

"Who?"

I took my eyes off the ceiling to glance at my mom. "She's the girl at my birth. The one you saw, and her name is Hypatia."

My mom's posture stiffened. "Ho—how could you possibly know that?"

I heaved a sigh. "It's hard to explain. I've been seeing her likeness in other people, then suddenly, I just blurted her name out."

Her eyelids slid closed, then popped wide open. "You're not making a bit of sense."

I rolled my head back and groaned. I couldn't make my mom grasp what I felt. She didn't have a phantom-like being inside her. Explanations were pointless, but I tried anyway. "It's like the power inside me is sending my brain messages. I see flashes of her chocolate-brown hair and her ocean-blue eyes in girls who look like her, but just today I learned her name."

My mom sat next to me and wrapped her arm around me. "Oh, honey, listen to what you're saying."

I jabbed a finger into my chest. "I feel her, and I think I should let the power guide me to the truth."

"You can't be serious," Mom blurted out, then raised her voice. "That sounds crazy. We'll find another way."

Was there another way? Did I have a choice? The power had already been doing what it wanted. Would pursuing Hypatia be any different? I didn't think so, but for my mom's sake, I lied. "You're probably right."

My mom's shoulders quivered as tears moistened her eyes. She quickly pulled herself together and said with conviction, "There is, I promise you." She rose from the bed and kissed the top of my head. "Good night."

"Good night." I waited for her to shut my door. Closing my eyes, I whispered, "Hypatia, where are you?"

****

The next morning, I threw every ounce of energy into my studies. I couldn't let thoughts of Hypatia get inside my head and distract me, but I *had* to think about her. She made me tremble all over, have sweaty palms, breathe faster, and plaster a goofy smile on my face. Overnight, I had become obsessed with her. I wanted to know how her hair smelled, feel the softness of her skin, hear her voice, gaze into her gorgeous eyes. How old was she? What was her connection to the power inside me? Had they been in love? Had something forced them apart? Were they searching for each other...for me? Rick's loud groan shattered my thoughts, and I peered over the worn binding of my English book. Absorbed in his journal and writing furiously across the page, he wrinkled his brow, pressing his pen to his lips. He looked up and caught me watching him. "Concentrate on your lesson, not me."

I needed a sounding board, and so far, Rick had been very open-minded to my circumstances. He could have some ideas as to how I could learn more about Hypatia. "Um, can I talk to you about something?"

"What's up?"

"Well, I...I saw this girl." I cleared my throat. "And I thought I knew her. I called her Hypatia." I shivered as I said her name.

Rick raised his eyebrows, then frowned. "That's a biblical name. Who names a kid Hypatia?"

I slammed the book closed and pushed it aside. "But this girl wasn't Hypatia, I only thought she was. I had a dream about her. Not about the girl, but Hypatia." I could feel the goofy smile spreading across my lips. "Hypatia is beautiful, and I can't stop thinking about her. I feel like I love her or the power does. I don't know."

Rick dropped his journal onto the floor. "You feel what?"

I lowered my voice and admitted, "I'm pretty sure the thing inside me loves her, or loved her, so now I feel what it feels."

He rubbed his palm over his mouth before saying, "So, there's some truth to Eve's words."

I flopped backward and sank into the couch. "I don't know, maybe. But her visions did confirm what my mom said. What I don't get is why almost 17 years later it decides to show itself."

"Back up. How can you be sure this Hypatia person is even real?"

I gave him a head bob. "Oh, she's real, and Eve said to let the power inside me guide me. Maybe it's looking for Hypatia. Maybe the dream I had wasn't my dream, but the power's."

"Could just be your subconscious," Rick offered.

"You just have to trust me on this one."

Rick leaned forward and kept his voice low. "If the entity, or as you say, the power, is pursuing this girl, then you have no choice but to pursue her as well."

I sighed. "I just want my life back."

Rick snapped his fingers. "What if this girl's searching for the power? What if they're both trying to find one another? Maybe if we find the girl, she'll know how to rid you of the power."

"But how?" I protested, throwing my hands up. "How do I find her?"

Rick stared at me for a moment. "I think Eve's right in saying the power will lead you to answers. It could lead you to this girl, and I think I've figured out the identity of the entity."

"What? Tell me!"

"I plugged all the indicators into Google and had it search for any relating material." He barked out a laugh. "The topic it came up with is out there, man. Are you sure you want to hear it?"

I gawked at him. "Yes! Of course, I want to hear it."

He sat very still, with his hands clasped in his lap. "Now remember, this is the internet."

"Just spit it out already!"

"Vampires," he said in one breath.

I blinked several times, then squinted at him. *What the...?*

"Hear me out. I took notes." He grabbed a legal pad out of his briefcase and began flipping through it. He stopped and tapped his finger against the page. "Okay, a vampire: a corpse that rises during the night, preys upon humans, and drains them of their blood."

"Hey now, I haven't done any of that stuff."

He gave me one of those "Really?" expressions before continuing. "The powers of vampires: supernatural sight, hearing, strength, the ability to read minds, and sending messages by thought." Rick paused, scanning the page. He looked up at me and said, "Listen to this. The sight and smell of blood awakens the vampire, sending him into a frenzy. Blood controls vampires, and they will stop at nothing to obtain it."

I scooted toward the edge of the couch. "Go on."

"The pulse of a human heartbeat can be heard from miles away by a vampire. The rhythm acts as a homing device to narrow in on the victim." He set the pad aside and gazed at me with focus. "Maybe you're attracted to blood and hear heartbeats because the entity inside you is a vampire."

The hair rose on the back of my neck. Acknowledging the possibility of a vampire inside of me was...well, nuts, and weren't they just a myth, a figment of imagination, a folktale? "I know I've done some creepy stuff, but a vampire? Do they even exist?"

"Hey, I've seen some bizarre things being a friend of Eve's. Besides, you got a better idea?"

I cocked my head and considered it. Truth was I didn't. "No."

"So then, if this girl—"

I cut him off and corrected him. "Hypatia."

"If Hypatia is linked to the power, then finding her is key."

I slowly shook my head. "Then I don't stand a chance. She could be anywhere."

Rick squeezed my shoulder. "Remember what Eve said, let the power lead you."

"Rick, I don't think I can do this alone. Will you help me?"

He didn't even hesitate. "You've got it, but we need a place to start. I can check with Eve, see if she can offer up something more on the girl." He pulled his eyebrows together and gave me a good, long stare. "And you should talk to your mom.

See if she will help too."

I shook my head hard. I could just picture her going off on me if I brought up the word vampire. "Not a good idea. She freaked out over Eve's reading. If I said there's a vampire inside me, she'd come unglued."

"I think it's a mistake, but I can't force you to talk to her."

"Will you still help me?"

He waited a long while before responding. "Yes."

****

Rick left shortly before we sat down for dinner. Dad rattled off a quick, "For life, for healing, for joy, we are thankful. Amen."

Mom mimicked, "Amen."

Lindsey was texting on her cell as she mumbled, "Amen."

"Amen," I said under my breath before spearing a piece of pork chop.

Dad gave Lindsey the arched brow look, and when she didn't respond, he belted out in his stern voice, "No phones at the dinner table."

Lindsey rolled her eyes and heaved a sigh. "Fine, but if I have to stay home one more day because of my stupid foot, I'll scream."

"It must be horrible staying home with your mom," Mom countered, then softly laughed.

"You know what I mean. I miss my friends."

"You'll be back soon enough," Dad commented, then swallowed a mouthful of pork before switching topics. "Diane, remind me to call Linda after dinner. I need budget totals from her first thing tomorrow morning."

Mom pushed her food around her plate as she gave him a nod.

If only I had such trivial things to worry about, but no, I had the burden of figuring out if a vampire was stuck inside my body. All I could think of was ridding myself of it. I needed to focus on that, not this meaningless chatter. I looked at my mom and blurted out, "Can I eat in my room?"

Mom's eyes grew large. "Why? What's wrong, Brandon?"

My dad looked me up and down with a furrowed brow.

"Are you not feeling well, son?"

Even Lindsey gave me a strange look.

"I'm fine. Just need to finish my homework." I lied but telling them I wanted to do vampire research on my computer was totally out.

"Homework?" Dad questioned. "Rick must have made an impression on you."

"Yeah, he's pretty cool. Can I be excused?"

Mom gave in. "Sure, honey."

"Thanks." Grabbing my plate, I left the table and jetted upstairs to my room. By the peaceful hum of my computer, I finished my dinner while searching vampire sites. As I flipped through images of fangs, blood, and words of insanity, the severity of it all sank in. Maybe Rick was right. Maybe talking to both my parents was the smart thing to do. I was in way over my head, and my parents always had my best interests at heart. They'd want to protect me. They'd want to rid me of this thing. I trusted them, so talking to them *was* the right thing. I scooped up my empty plate and trekked downstairs into the kitchen. Dad was helping Mom with the dishes.

I set mine by the sink and took a deep breath. "Can I talk to you guys?"

Mom wiped her hands on a dish towel, giving me her full attention. "Of course."

"What's up?" Dad asked in a lighthearted tone.

I pointed to the barstools. "Maybe you guys should sit down."

My mom neared me. "Why, Brandon?" My dad joined her at her side.

My gaze ping-ponged between them as I said, "I think I know what's wrong with me, but it's way out there."

My mom's body stiffened as she stared me down. She didn't want my dad to learn about the girl, the mist, and Eve, but I didn't care anymore. "I need to say this. You have to let me say this, but I need you both to promise not to freak out."

"What's this about?" Dad asked, his tone growing serious.

"Promise," I pressed.

"We promise," Dad agreed. "Now, tell us."

I decided to just spit it out. "Rick did some research and he—we believe the power inside me may be a vampire."

My mom stumbled back a step, then latched onto my dad's arm. His mouth fell open, then he gave his head a good shake as if to clear it.

"You promised, remember?"

Dad jerked his head to face Mom. "Rick told our son he's a vampire!"

Mom let out a quick high-pitched bark of laughter, then attempted damage control. "Mike, it's okay. Brandon's under a lot of pressure right now. He's not thinking clearly."

"What the hell is wrong with that man? No one in their right mind would say such a thing." Dad's face turned bright red as he sliced his hand through the air. "That's it, I don't want him around Brandon. Or, dear God, Lindsey. Rick is no longer welcome in our home."

The power inside me surged, and my muscles flexed with a strength I knew wasn't my own. Adrenaline thrust me toward my dad. I pointed a finger in his face and yelled, "You can't tell me what to do. I make my own rules. Rick stays!"

My dad raised his hand to strike but held it in midair as he warned, "Brandon, don't you dare speak to me in that tone."

I snatched his hand in a grip-lock, squeezing harder and harder, not letting go until he cried out and buckled to his knees. "I'll use whatever tone I like."

My mom knelt at his side, shielding him from me. Her gaze darted upward, locking with mine. "Brandon, what is wrong with you?"

Her words meant nothing; my focus was their blood-filled veins, pulsating at 90 miles an hour. Was that fear? If so, the power within felt no remorse. My dad had angered it, and it retaliated, not me. I had no control over my own actions. Couldn't they see that? The power's demands flew out of my mouth, "Rick stays or I go."

My dad threw a cold, hard glare my way as he rose to his feet. He offered his hand to my mom and helped her up, yet his eyes never left mine. "I have no idea what has gotten into you, Brandon, but you do not make the rules in this house. Is that clear?"

I glanced at my mom, knowing the power's dominance would shine through my eyes. She would see it. She would know it wasn't me.

My mom's face turned pale white. Had she caught a glimpse of its strength? "Wait!" Mom called out. "Mike, maybe we should give Rick a chance to explain."

He swung his head in her direction as if she were insane. "This is not our son. This is Rick's doing."

Mom had kept my dad in the dark about everything, past and present. Now he blamed Rick, and that was her fault. Mom trembled as she spoke. "We don't know that."

"What possible explanation could make this right?" Dad argued. "My decision is final. Rick goes."

I slammed my fist into the wall and fled the kitchen before either of them could speak. I didn't stop running until I shut myself off in my room. Heaves rippled through my chest as I burst into tears. The power, vampire, whatever its title, was destroying my life. The whoosh of the door opening filtered through my sobs. "Go away," I shouted, before jumping on my bed and burying my face into my pillow.

Footsteps brushed over the carpet, then Mom's voice filled my ears. "What's going on with you? You've never acted with such disrespect." I felt her sit next to me on my bed. "Is your father right? Is Rick putting ideas into your head?"

I turned toward her and cried, "Rick's the only one who gets it, and if Dad makes him leave, I'll have no one."

"That's not true, honey." She stroked my back. "You have us, your family. I know Rick means well, but vampires?" Again, she let out a nervous cackle. "That's just nonsense. They don't exist."

I sat up and twisted the edge of my pillow between my fingers. "How do you know that?"

She lifted a single eyebrow. "Well, because...they're a myth."

"You of all people should believe," I threw at her. "I mean, you went on about some girl and mist that no one else saw."

"You're right, maybe I should be more open, but the fact is I did see a girl, a human being."

I mocked her. "And mist enter me."

"Brandon, I love you, but I refuse to believe that my son is possessed by a vampire. If you must hold on to this silly belief, then keep it to yourself, and especially from your father."

I latched onto her arm. "And Rick? Please, Mom, can he stay?"

Her voice sounded exhausted and troubled. "He can stay until I find a replacement, and even that will be a hard sell with your father." Her gaze lingered on me for several seconds, then she hurried out of my room.

I stared at the closed door as the empty silence in my room consumed me. Had the power just stripped me of my parents? Was I alone in this mess now? I chucked the pillow across the room as the painful sobs returned.

CHAPTER 9

The next morning when Rick arrived, my mom whisked him off into the den. Their muffled voices were barely audible behind the closed door. I crept up to the door and pressed my ear against its frame, straining to catch a word here or there.

"Whatcha doing?"

Lindsey's voice made me jerk away from the door. My lips spread into one of those automatic busted grins, then I shoved my hands into my pockets. "Nothing."

She bobbed her chin toward the den. "Uh-uh. You were eavesdropping. Spill."

I put my finger to my lips. "Shh."

She crossed her arms and huffed. "Don't shush me."

I faced her head-on, then did a double take. She stood crutchless, tapping her foot. "When did you lose the crutches?"

"Yesterday, and don't try to change the subject."

I hadn't even noticed. Then again, I did have a crapload of my own problems to deal with.

"Well?"

I glanced at the door, then back at Lindsey. "Mom and Dad want to ax Rick. Mom's in there with Rick now."

"What? Why?"

I waved her away. "You don't wanna know."

She socked me in the arm. "Of course, I do!"

The door swung open, shelving my response. Mom stepped into the hallway as she said, "Thank you, Rick." She stopped at my side, then squeezed my shoulder before heading upstairs.

Lindsey centered her big green orbs on me. "What happened?"

I ignored her and rushed into the den. Rick's somber expression stopped me dead in my tracks. Lindsey came in seconds behind and planted herself beside Rick.

"I'm sorry," I offered up, knowing an apology wasn't enough. "I told them. I thought maybe...but I was wrong. I should've stuck to my gut."

He shrugged it off. "It's not your fault, but this does pose a problem as my replacement could come any day now. We'll have to work fast to find answers."

"Okay, yeah."

He lowered his voice. "I may have stumbled onto something."

"Will somebody please tell me what's going on?" Lindsey demanded.

"Keep your voice down," I urged, pointing to the open door. "Go close the door."

Lindsey hurried over and pushed it closed. "Well?"

I hesitated, gauging how to word it, but her wide-eyed expression radiated enthusiasm, so I didn't hold back. "I told Mom and Dad that Rick and I think the power inside me might be a vampire. They pretty much freaked out. Now they're letting Rick go."

Her eyes grew even larger as she uttered, "Vampire?" She slumped onto the couch and scooped up a pillow, hugging it tight.

"It makes sense, Lins." I sat next to her and rested my hand on her shoulder. "With everything that's happened, it makes sense."

She sat still, staring straight ahead, then glanced at me and whispered, "I don't think they're real."

"That's what we're gonna find out," Rick pointed out.

"You can't tell Mom and Dad," I insisted.

She gave a quick head bob. "No, of course not."

I faced Rick. "So, what did you stumble on?"

He shuffled through his briefcase and pulled out a few sheets of paper. He kept his voice scarcely above a whisper as he said, "I found a couple sites where inside the chatrooms, people claimed to be actual vampires. Here, like this guy, who stated he doesn't require blood, that red food coloring works just as well and makes him feel less guilty."

Lindsey smothered her face into the pillow and burst out laughing.

I pursed my lips at Lindsey, then focused my attention on Rick. "That sounds more like a freak than a vampire."

He plastered a smirk on his face. "Thank you, Captain Obvious."

Lindsey nudged my arm. "Yeah, Captain Obvious."

I shrugged it off. "So, what's your point then?"

"What I was getting at is that his statement lacks credibility. No one can survive on food coloring, and vampires don't strike me as creatures that feel guilty." Rick tapped the sheet of paper. "Now, this statement carries some weight. He says, and I quote, 'I keep my victims alive to savor a pint of delicious blood each day. I thrive on the fear in their eyes. It seeps out in salty tears that taste like wine, and the more I laugh, the more they cry. Yum, yum, your blood on my tongue.' I'd hate to come across that guy in a dark alley."

Lindsey latched onto my arm. "Oh my God, that's super creepy."

Even I shuddered. "That guy really sounds like a vampire."

"Exactly," Rick said. "See the difference?"

The door opened, and our mom poked her head in.

"Lindsey, this isn't social hour. Brandon's in class. Out."

"But Mom..."

"Don't 'but mom' me." She wiggled her finger toward her. "Out."

Lindsey groaned, then tossed the pillow aside. "Fine."

"See ya, Lins."

She flashed me a "You better fill me in later" look before sulking out the door.

I waited a good 30 seconds to make sure my mom wasn't coming back, then I grabbed my laptop. "I'm gonna do a Google search for vampire chatrooms."

"There's a lot out there, and most are absurd."

As the first page loaded, I blinked. "There's over two million sites!"

"Just stick to the first page."

"Good idea." I randomly selected Vampire Chat. Not the most original title, but hey, what did I know? With a few keystrokes, I set up my username and password, provided my email address and posted my picture. "Click here to enter" flashed on the screen. I did, and a dark red list of members appeared. I glanced at Rick. "I'm in."

Within seconds, Bloodrose sent me my first message. "Hey, cutie. Your blood isn't the only thing I want to suck."

My face grew incredibly hot, and I couldn't log out fast enough.

Rick chuckled. "Your face is beet-red. What'd they say?"

I cleared my throat. "Um...nothing that's gonna help. I don't think this is the right chatroom. Moving on." I scanned down the page, carefully reading the blurb of each site. "This might not be so easy."

Rick wheeled closer and peeked around my shoulder. "Well, for starters, eliminate all the ones with vampire chat in their title. I think a true vampire site would be more... superior."

I turned my laptop toward him. "You pick."

He flashed a proud smirk and rattled off, "Reign of Blood, Les Vampires, and Origin of the Undead look promising."

I sighed and threw my hands in the air. "How did you do that?"

"Doesn't matter. Just check 'em out." He glanced at the door. "We need to get into your lesson too."

"What? How am I supposed to concentrate on school?"

His tone turned unyielding. "I'm your teacher, and my first priority is your education."

"Geez, you sound like my parents."

"It matters, Brandon, especially now since they don't trust me. You've got a few more minutes to search the sites while I put your lesson together."

I settled back on the couch and grumbled, "I guess I don't have a choice."

"No, you don't."

I rolled my eyes before giving in and starting with Reign of Blood. It was more of a fact zone.

Vampintheknow posted: *The first vampire started out as not a vampire at all, but as a human man named Ambrogio. He was an Italian-born adventurer.*

Bloodyquotes posted: *The association with bats primarily comes from Bram Stoker's Dracula. But bats have always been a symbol of darkness and evil. And, of course, the vampire bat does drink blood.*

Vampirefacts posted: *The Alnwick Castle vampire predates the term "vampire." The events were recorded by an English chronicler named William of Newburgh. He reported the story of a man who returned from the dead as a revenant—a walking, rotting corpse—spreading plague in his wake.*

Countfacts posted: *Elizabeth Bathory is perhaps the most famous vampire in history after Vlad the Impaler. In the 16th century, she may have actually enjoyed torturing peasants, feeding on them, and bathing in their blood.*

Vampire history I didn't need, so I logged out and entered Origin of the Undead. Again, more facts. Next up, Les Vampires. No thrills or gimmicks greeted me, just an eerie pitch-black wall with a single word in red, *Bloodletting*, so I clicked on it.

"Yes?" appeared on the screen.

A chill crept over my flesh as I typed, "Are vampires real?"

"Why do you ask?"

I avoided answering their question and asked another. "Are you a vampire?"

I stared at my monitor, waiting. No reply came. Again, I typed, "Are you a vampire?"

The door to the den opened, and my mom entered. I logged out with a click of my finger, giving her a casual, "What's up?"

She closed the door behind her and centered her gaze on Rick. In a voice that reeked of politeness, she said, "Rick, the agency was able to find a tutor who can start tomorrow."

My stomach clenched. *No, it was too soon.* "Mom, please," I begged, "let Rick stay just a couple more days."

Rick nodded, then calmly said, "I understand."

"Thank you, Rick." Mom gave me a slight smile before leaving the room.

"It's too soon," I cried. "We need more time."

"It'll be okay, Brandon. You haven't lost me." He pulled a business card from his briefcase and scribbled on the back of it. "This is my cell. We can keep in touch this way."

I shoved the card into my pocket and shook my head. "Don't ask me to study now. I can't. All I can think about is that you're leaving."

"I'm not going to quit until we find the answer, I promise you."

****

I couldn't sit around the dinner table that night after my parents had kicked Rick out. This time, I didn't even ask when I had gotten up from the table and took my dinner to my room. They needed to see my disapproval, and hopefully, it would force them into one hefty guilt trip and they'd reverse their decision.

As I sat isolated inside my bedroom, a surge of tears threatened to spill over my eyes, but crying wasn't going to fix anything. It wouldn't bring Rick back or change my parents' minds. I swiped at my eyes, killing the waterworks, then glanced at my dinner plate. A whiff of grilled hamburger and salty French fries shattered my self-pity. I pushed aside the garden salad and took a huge bite of the burger, washing it down with a swig of Coke. I popped a couple fries into my mouth before flipping open my laptop. Les Vampires' pitch-black wall emerged with a blinking *Bloodletting* beckoning me to enter. I didn't hesitate to accept.

The anonymous person replied before my finger left the keyboard. "I see you have returned."

"Because I want an answer to my question."

"As I recall, my question was also unanswered."

I smirked at the screen. If this person thought they'd get the upper hand, they were sadly mistaken. "Answer mine, then I'll answer yours."

"I'm not interested in playing games with you. Answer my question or I'll end the communication."

Their reply popped my confidence like a balloon. Immediately, I surrendered. "No, wait, please. I'll answer you."

"Very well."

"I asked if vampires are real because..." My fingers paused, hovering over the keys. "I think I have one inside of me."

Several seconds of blackness met my gaze. My pulse climbed as I bounced my foot against the floor. "C'mon already," I shouted at the monitor.

As if my pen pal had heard, their reply flashed before me. "Tell me why you think this."

"I...I get urges."

"What kind of urges?"

"Non-human ones."

"I'm not here to play 20 questions."

"Blood urges." I hit the keys extra hard as I typed. "The smell forces me to hurt people, and heartbeats pound inside my head so loud, I can't concentrate."

"What brought on these cravings? Have you exchanged blood with another?"

I blinked, then read it again. *Exchanged blood?* I answered as honestly as I could. "I don't really know what you mean by 'exchanged,' but I don't think I've done that. When I was born, I was infected or changed by..." My fingers stumbled on the keyboard. "...mist. There was a girl, Hypatia, with brown hair and blue eyes with the mist."

Again, they hesitated before responding. "Tell me how you came to know this name?"

"The power inside me knows it. I think it loves, or loved her."

Words appeared, filling my screen. "You must go to a club called Bloodthirst. The location is 1137 Haven Avenue, Castle Beach, California. This is no ordinary club. Vampires run it. Ask for Margarete. Tell her you are looking for Hypatia. A word of caution: do not accept a vampire's kiss."

I broke out in a cold sweat and swallowed the lump in my throat. "Who is this?"

A dark screen stared back.

Again, I typed, "Who is this?"

No reply came, so I slammed my laptop shut. A vampire club? Who was Margarete? A vampire? Could I trust the words of a mystery person I'd met inside a vampire chatroom? And how could I pull off a trip to Castle Beach? My parents would never allow it. I slouched against the chair and sat there, staring at nothing.

When I finally pushed to my feet, drained of energy, I shuffled over to my bed and flopped on top of it. A beautiful voice humming that same soft, sweet lullaby from my childhood began to play inside my head. Just like when I was a kid, my eyelids grew heavy and I dozed off. Between that realm of consciousness and sleep, I felt something brush against my cheek. I bolted upright, scanning the length of my room and caught a glimpse of a gray silhouette drifting past my window. "Hypatia?" I whispered, scooting to the end of my bed and peering at the window.

No response came, but I had to be sure and ran to the light, flipping it on. The curtains draped over the window met my vision, nothing more. I fell back onto my bed and heaved a sigh. "I'm losing it," I said, focusing on the ceiling and tracing the knots in the wooden beams. Several minutes later, my eyelids slid closed once more.

A hand squeezed my shoulder, then shook me. "Hypatia?" I mumbled.

Mom's voice filled my ears. "Brandon, you need to get up. The new tutor will be here soon."

I rubbed my eyes, then squinted up at her. "What time is it?"

She opened my curtains. "Seven-thirty. You've got a half hour."

I threw the covers aside, humming the lullaby, then paused and cocked my head. "Mom, were you in my room last night?"

She wrinkled her brow. "No, why?"

"Um...no reason." If my mom hadn't been the one humming or the one who'd touched me, then who had?

"Hurry up then and get ready." She gathered up my laundry. "I'll have your breakfast waiting in the kitchen."

"Okay." Maybe it was Lindsey's ghost. I smirked, waving the stupid thought away and headed for the shower.

After throwing on a pair of jeans and a T-shirt, I jogged downstairs and into the kitchen. My mom had set a plate of French toast smothered in maple syrup and a large glass of orange juice on the island for me. Lindsey was halfway through with hers when I sat down. "Back to school?"

Lindsey released a big sigh. "Finally." She stopped and studied me. "This is your first day without Rick. Are you okay?"

I shoved a forkful of French toast into my mouth. "No, but there's not much I can do about it."

She flattened her lips before saying, "Mom and Dad cancelling Rick was messed up."

I leaned in and whispered, "I got his cell. We're still working the vampire angle."

She high-fived me. "Awesome. Whatever the plan, I'm in."

"Thanks, Lins."

The doorbell sang out, demanding attention. "I got it," Mom called from somewhere toward the front of the house.

Seconds later, a hint of musky copper spiked the air. I jerked my head in the direction of the scent as warm sweat coated my palms.

"What's wrong?" Lindsey asked, her voice muffled and distant.

I gathered every ounce of energy to restrain the power, then uttered, "Blood...I smell blood."

She gripped my shoulder and ordered, "Stay here. Don't move."

Her feet pounding against the floor echoed inside my ears. I gripped the edge of the island, fighting off the power's thirst as the thick, salty aroma baited me.

Mom's soft voice filled my head. "Brandon, what's wrong?"

I inched my head around to view her fuzzy outline standing next to me. "They're not safe," I answered as I licked my lips. "Make them leave."

"Why?" Mom pressed.

"Just do it, Mom," Lindsey blurted out in a shrill voice.

"Lindsey, calm down. Brandon, what's going on?"

Specks of red blurred my vision as I forced out each word. "I...can...smell...blood."

"Blood?" Mom sounded confused.

"As soon as you opened the door, he freaked out." Lindsey clued Mom in. "It has to be the new tutor." "Stay with Brandon. I'll be right back." "It'll be okay," Lindsey assured.

I was less convinced and gripped the counter, terrified if I let go, I'd dash after the scent I craved and devour it. I couldn't hurt another person. Then, the bloody odor just vanished seconds before Mom walked into the kitchen.

An unfocused look claimed Mom's face as she said, "She had a paper cut, so I told her there'd been a mistake and sent her on her way." Mom's eyes found mine. "This is going to keep happening, isn't it—this blood compulsion of yours?"

I flinched as if she'd slapped me, then lowered my gaze to the floor. "I'm sorry."

Lindsey came to my defense. "Mom, he can't help it."

"Stay out of this, Lindsey," Mom scolded before blowing out an exasperated breath. "Go get your backpack. We need to get going."

"But Mom, Brandon needs—"

"Let me worry about Brandon. You need to get to school. Go on, get your stuff so we can get going."

"Whatever," Lindsey groaned, stomping off.

I glanced upward, slowly meeting my mom's eyes. Her expression softened as she said, "I'm at a loss, Brandon. I haven't the slightest clue what's going on, let alone how to solve it. I have no choice but to ask Rick back. I'll call him from the car." She hugged me tight, like she'd never let go, then left the room without another word.

As the front door slammed shut, I counted to 10 before racing to the living room window and peeking out. Mom's car backed out of the driveway, and when it disappeared down the street, I thrust my fists in the air and did a victory lap around the sofa. "Thank God for the paper cut." Ten minutes later, I hit up Rick's cell.

"Hello?"

"It's Brandon. Has my mom called you yet?"

"Just got off the phone with her. I'm headed to your house right now. What happened?"

"The new tutor had a paper cut, and I—"

"Smelled the blood," Rick said, finishing my sentence.

"Yeah, but my mom's definitely not happy."

"I got that from our phone call. We'll work it out. I'll be there in a few."

"Awesome."

Every time a car got within earshot of our house, I bolted to the window, searching for Rick. I could hardly wait to get his take on the conversation I had inside the chatroom. When I finally heard tires hit our driveway, I raced to the door, only to find my mom on the other side with her keys in her hand.

She raised her brows. "Expecting someone?"

"You know I am."

"I get it. You're excited to have Rick back, but you need to focus on your studies and not these ridiculous theories."

"They're not any more ridiculous than what you told me," I challenged her.

A serious expression pulled her face taut. "I mean it, Brandon, and I'm going to have a hell of a time trying to explain this to your father."

I held up my hands in surrender. "Fine, I'll focus on school, I promise."

The doorbell rang, and I lunged for it, but my mom blocked my path. She held up a firm hand like a crossing guard. "I'll get it."

I shoved my hands into my pockets and shrugged like it was no big deal. "Fine."

She gave me that raised brow look of hers, then pulled the door open. "Hello, Rick." Her tone was on the cool side.

"Please, come in."

Rick didn't seem affected as he rattled off a chipper, "Good morning, Mrs. Cass."

She stepped in front of his wheelchair and placed her hands on her hips. "As I said to my son, you're here to teach, nothing more. Do I make myself clear?"

He gave a quick nod. "Crystal."

"Very well." She moved aside, allowing him to pass. "Rick, would you like some coffee?"

"Yes, that would be great. Thank you."

"I just got back from dropping Lindsey off at school. I'll start a fresh pot and bring you a cup when it's ready."

"Thank you."

"Welcome." She gave a slight smile, then left us alone in the hallway.

Rick and I headed to the den without making eye contact, but once inside its four walls, and with the door safely settled into its frame, we engaged. In a tone off Mom's radar, I let my words fly. "Oh my God, Rick, you're not going to believe this. I think I chatted with a real vampire. I mean, they seemed real. I think they were real. Yeah, they were real!"

Cracking a smile, he said, "Slow down. Take a deep breath and start over." He dug into his briefcase, pulled out several sheets of paper and an algebra book while keeping his gaze on me.

I plopped down on the couch, blew out several deep breaths, then enlightened him. "That chatroom, Les Vampires, well, it's for real, and the person didn't waste time, got right to the point, and asked direct questions. Once

I told them about Hypatia, they gave me the name of a club." I leaned forward and whispered, "A *vampire* club. Told me to ask for Margarete."

Rick fell back in his chair, unleashing the algebra book into his lap. "Jesus."

"There's more. Last night in my room, I'm sure I heard humming, then someone touched me." I paused and locked eyes with him. "I think it was Hypatia."

He kept his voice low, but his words jumped with excitement. "What? How is that even possible?"

I shrugged. "I don't know, but she was in my room, I'm sure of it."

He gripped the wheels of his chair and zipped over to me. "You know what this means, right?" He didn't wait for my reply. "It means we've got to check out this club."

My mom came in with a steaming mug of coffee. Luckily, the algebra book saved the day as Rick handed it to me and said, "Chapters 7 and 8 are our focus today."

Mom seemed convinced, as she offered up a pleasant smile and handed Rick his coffee. "Sounds fun." For show, I let out a groan.

She tousled my hair and teased, "You'll get through it." Her good-humored mood faded, and she replaced it with a much more serious 'I mean business' tone as she said, "Since Lindsey's restricted to half-days, I'll be leaving at noon to pick her up from school. Can I trust you to behave while I'm gone?"

"Mom, c'mon, I'm not a kid."

She arched her famous brow at me. "You know what I mean."

"We'll focus on lessons, Mrs. Cass," Rick assured with a confident nod.

She regarded us for a brief second. "Very well. I'll let you guys get to work."

After she closed the door, I fell back on the couch and sighed. "She's gonna stalk me for sure."

Rick's facial muscles clenched. "I'm not okay with lying to her, but unfortunately, I don't see another way."

"There isn't another way. My parents made sure of that."

He rubbed his chin and gave a slow nod. "Well then, it's time to plan a course of action."

****

Rick and I were thick into our strategy when Lindsey barged into the den. I snapped my laptop shut and groaned.

"Do you knock?"

"You're up to something." She grabbed my laptop and flipped it open, blinked, then her eyes doubled in size. "A vampire club? I'm so in."

I snatched it back and tucked it behind me. "No way, Lins. Mom and Dad would kill me."

She threw up her hands. "They'll freak either way. I'm going!"

"I have to side with Brandon on this one," Rick chimed in. "It's too dangerous, Lindsey."

Her gaze darted between us, then she centered her full attention on me, squeezing my hand. "You're my brother. I'm not letting you do this alone."

"He won't be alone," Rick assured. "I'll be with him."

"What if something goes wrong? You guys need me."

A thick wrinkle creased Rick's brow. "She might be right." He pointed at his legs. "I mean, how much help can I be?"

Lindsey flashed a proud smile. "See, told ya."

"I don't mean your help, Lindsey," Rick said with a firm nod, "but we should look into finding a third person we can trust."

She crossed her arms and huffed. "You're not gonna find someone."

"And I didn't say you could go either," I pointed out.

"Did I *say* I was asking?" Lindsey bit back, then smirked.

"I could be a narc and spill your plans to Mom and Dad."

I rolled my eyes and heaved a long-suffering sigh. "You're such a spoiled brat."

"And you're just jealous."

"Hey now, hold it down, you two," Rick interjected. "The last thing we need is for your mom to come running in here." He turned to Lindsey. "Maybe you could let us off the hook and stay home."

She stared him down with a narrowed gaze. "No way."

He forced a laugh, then shrugged. "Okay then. It appears Lindsey is coming along."

Lindsey quietly clapped her hands, then sank into Dad's recliner as her lips spread into a huge smile.

I waved her away, focusing on Rick. "Since we're stuck with her, might as well tell her the plan."

"Agreed. So, here's the plan. No phones, no luggage, backpacks only. We'll pay with all cash, no credit cards and no car. We'll travel by bus."

"I can't bring my cell?" she asked, her voice growing smaller.

"The moment your parents realize you're gone, they'll call the police. We can't bring anything that can be traced back to us if we want this mission to be successful."

She gave me that panicked look. "But Mom and Dad will worry. They'll think something happened to us."

I wrapped my arm around her shoulder. "I'm going to leave a note, let them know we're okay." Her body jumped slightly.

"Stay home, Lins, please," I begged. "This has nothing to do with you, and I'd never forgive myself if something happened to you."

She splayed her fingers across her chest. "It has everything to do with me because you're my brother. We have each other's backs, remember? I'm coming."

Rick clapped his hands, interrupting us. "We've already established Lindsey's joining us. No sense in rehashing."

"About the bus tickets, Lins and I get an allowance, but—"

Rick cut me off. "I've got a friend at Goldline Transit. He owes me a favor. Tickets won't be a problem. What we need to decide is when do we leave."

"I guess that depends on how fast you can get the tick-ets," I pointed out.

"Right." Rick nodded. "I'll text him now with all the info. He'll give me an answer on when."

Lindsey and I sat motionless, our gazes fixated on Rick's cell. A few minutes passed and my breath hitched inside my throat, then Rick looked up and grinned. "Says I can have tickets by tonight for tomorrow's fare. Leaves at midnight to Castle Beach." He raised his brows. "Are we in?"

I glanced at Lindsey. She gave me a quick head bob. "We're in."

"Okay, I'm texting back a thumbs-up."

My stomach twisted into knots as my journey just be-came reality.

"YOLO," Lindsey whispered.

"Yeah," I whispered back.

"We're on for tomorrow night," Rick confirmed. "I'll catch a cab your way, but we should meet a couple blocks away from your house. Let's say on the corner of Wellford and Canvas at 11?"

"Yeah, Lins and I can walk there."

"What about money?" Lindsey asked. "I mean, we'll have to stay somewhere when we get there, right?"

"We'll bring what we've saved from our allowance," I told her.

"I'll stop at the bank when I leave here and take out plenty of cash, so don't worry," Rick reassured her. "And remember, pack light. Just what will fit in your backpacks."

CHAPTER 10

As I placed the note to our parents on my dresser, Lindsey tiptoed into my room, suited up in a purple hoodie, jeans, and flowered sneakers. She hugged her backpack to her chest as her gaze circled my room.

"You ready?" I asked.

"I took these from Mom's jewelry box." She opened her palm, revealing two cross necklaces. She slipped one around her neck and put the other around mine.

"What's this for?"

A dead serious look pulled at her face. "We need to protect ourselves." She unzipped her backpack and angled it toward me. "I also raided Dad's workshop in the garage. Found these skinny pieces of wood. We can use them as stakes."

I snickered, then pushed the pack closed. "Really, Lins?"

"Do *you* know anything about vampires or what they're capable of? I don't."

"Well, since one might be inside me, I think I've got one up on you."

"And look what you've done. A real vampire may do worse."

"Fine. Bring 'em."

She gave me a cocky nod. "You'll thank me later." The note on my dresser drew her eye. "You didn't tell them I forced you to take me with, did you?"

"Mom and Dad's wrath for just me going is gonna be bad enough. No way am I letting them think I agreed to let you tag along." I paused. "You know, you could just stay home."

"Would you quit saying that!"

"Whatever," I grumbled, tossing my pack over my shoulder and heading for the door. I glanced back at her. "Are you coming?"

She dashed to my side, her chin quivering and her eyes filling with tears as she hugged me and whispered, "I'm not gonna let anything happen to you."

I hugged her back. "Nothing's gonna happen to me. You can't get rid of me that easily."

She pulled away, snorted out a laugh, then wiped her nose. "Promise?"

"I promise. Now, we gotta go or we'll be late meeting Rick."

She sniffled a couple more times before nodding.

I cracked my bedroom door and pressed my ear to the opening. The thump of my heart bounced inside my head as I listened to the utter stillness of the hallway; a good sign our parents had gone to bed. But just to be on the safe side, I peeked out, sweeping my gaze up and down a vacant second floor. I gave Lindsey a thumbs-up and waved her forward. In the dark, we crept down the stairs and slipped out the front door like a pair of thieves.

When we reached the driveway, we bolted, sprinting down the street. The crisp night air stung my cheeks and turned my breaths into puffs of fog, but I didn't stop running.

As I crossed Whitter, I latched onto Lindsey's arm and skidded her to a stop, before spinning around and scanning the dimly lit street. Other than a couple of cats, the street was empty.

Lindsey glanced over her shoulder. "I think we're good."

I shoved my hands into my pockets to warm them up. "Yeah, we can walk the rest of the way."

"Are you scared?" she asked, pushing her hoodie off her head and letting her hair fall free.

Laughter slipped out before I could force it back down. "Yeah, maybe a little. You?"

"Yes," she breathed, then shoved her hand in my face.

"Don't say it. I'm not going home."

"I got it, Lins. I'm stuck with you whether I like it or not."

"Totally."

"Seriously though, you need to listen to me. Stick by my side and do what I say," I attempted Dad's stern tone. "I'm responsible for your safety. You can't be...you know...you."

She anchored a hand on her hip and huffed. "What's that supposed to mean?"

I waved her away. "Don't act clueless. You know exactly what I'm talking about. You might be Dad's princess, but not the world's."

She pursed her lips. "Fine. Whatever."

"I'm not doing this to be a jerk. I'm doing this to protect you."

Her expression softened, and she offered me a slight smile. "I know."

"Brandon, over here," Rick called out.

I turned away from Lindsey and glanced in the direction of Rick's voice. My gaze spotted a cab parked on Welford, underneath a cluster of trees. Rick was leaning out of it, waving us over. I nudged Lindsey's arm, and we headed for the cab. As Rick pushed the door open, the sheen from a streetlight illuminated a silver cross hanging around his neck.

I rolled my eyes. "Really? You're as bad as Lindsey."

Lindsey patted her backpack. "I brought stakes too."

He dug into his pack and revealed the tip of a carved piece of wood. "Me too. Never can be too careful." I fell back against the seat, groaning.

Rick tapped the glass separating us from the cab driver. "We're ready."

The driver nodded and gunned the engine, jetting away from the curb and thrusting the three of us against the back seat.

As we zipped down the street, Rick handed Lindsey and I our bus tickets. "I also booked two rooms at the Sleeptime Lodge," he said. "It's on the same street as Bloodthirst."

"I thought you said no credit cards," Lindsey pointed out.

"Apparently, you don't need one to reserve a room there. Not sure what that says about the hotel, but we'll find out soon enough."

Lindsey wrinkled her nose. "Probably means it's a dump."

"This isn't a vacation," Rick threw back at her. "Accommodations don't matter."

"To you, maybe."

As I listened to the two of them bicker, I closed my eyes and dozed off. Inside my dream, Hypatia floated toward me, humming that same lullaby. Her ruby red lips spread into a beautiful smile, which turned deadly as she revealed her pointy, polished fangs, dripping with fresh blood. Something wet trickled down my neck, and I swiped it with my hand. A gasp rushed up my throat as I pulled away bloodstained fingers. It was *my* blood! She bit me! She wasn't a girl at all, she was a vampire. I stumbled backward and belted out a high-pitched scream.

Hands reached inside my dream, shaking me, then Rick's loud voice echoed in my ears. "Brandon! Wake up!"

My eyelids flew open. I grabbed Rick's arm and blurted out, "Oh my God."

Rick, Lindsey, and even the cab driver had that wide-eyed stare plastered on their faces.

"Talk to me," Rick pressed. "Are you okay?"

"Yeah. I think so."

"Really, are you okay?" Lindsey questioned.

Hypatia's bloodstained fangs flashed inside my brain and I shivered, shaking off the image. "I'm okay." The cab driver's gaze remained transfixed in his rearview mirror on me. He seemed to need an explanation, so I offered, "Bad dream."

"Had a few of those myself," he empathized, then returned his focus to the street.

I waved Rick and Lindsey closer, whispering, "I'm pretty sure Hypatia's a vampire."

Rick jerked his head back, then demanded an explanation. "How can you possibly know that?"

"Vampire?" Lindsey repeated, scrunching her brows together. "Wait, who's Hypatia?"

I looked back and forth between them. "She showed me her fangs, and...bit me."

Rick closed his eyes as he shook his head, then gave me a blank look. "You're not making sense."

"Well, not literally," I pointed out. "She did it in the dream I just had."

Rick put his hand on my shoulder and gave a feeble grin. "You've been through a lot. It's understandable that your subconscious most likely conquered up her image as a vampire." I jabbed a finger into my chest. "No, I *felt* her."

"Dreams can be very vivid and very real. Studies have shown—"

"It wasn't a damn dream!" I blurted out, cutting him off.

"Calm down," Rick urged, glancing toward the driver.

"I believe you," Lindsey said softly. "But who is Hypatia?"

The driver's voice bellowed past the perforated glass. "Everything okay back there?"

Rick offered up his hand in an apologetic manner. "All good."

The deep lines of suspicion creasing the driver's forehead stifled my claims to a response. Raising questions was the last thing we needed. I shoved my emotions down my throat and sank into my seat, turning my attention to Lindsey. "She's linked to the power inside me."

She squeezed my hand. "That makes me believe you even more."

Maybe it wasn't so bad having her along. I gave her a heartfelt smile. "Thanks, Lins."

"The bus terminal, folks," the driver announced as he swung his cab into the entrance. He rolled to a stop next to the loading and unloading passenger zone, then shut off the meter. "That'll be an even $45."

Rick handed him cash. "Thank you."

"Welcome." He collected Rick's chair off the back before opening the passenger door. "Do you need any help?"

"No, thanks. I've got it," Rick replied, gripping the wheelchair arms and sliding onto the seat.

"Very well. You kids take care now."

As the yellow car sped off, Rick angled his wheelchair in front of me, blocking my path. "We need to be careful, Brandon, and not draw attention to ourselves. You can't just blurt things out where others can hear you."

I crossed my arms and gave him a hefty scowl. "You have no idea what I'm going through or how I feel, so don't tell me how I should act."

Lindsey touched my arm. "Brandon, it's okay. Rick's just trying to help."

"I don't know how you feel," Rick admitted, "but what I do know is we have to be smart and careful or all of this will fall apart."

The sting of angry tears blurred my vision. "I just want my life back."

Rick gripped my hand and gave it a firm squeeze. "And we're gonna get it back."

"I hope so," I mumbled.

Lindsey hugged me tight and laced her voice with the strength I needed. "We will, Brandon."

Rick tapped his watch. "We're supposed to board the bus 15 minutes before departure. We should get going."

Lindsey smirked and slapped my arm, returning to her bratty self. "Yeah, slacker."

"Nice, Lins."

She strutted after Rick, waving me off. I dissed her back and centered my attention on our bus. A stocky, musclebound driver with thinning hair stood leaning against a large, gray-colored bus. He collected our tickets before placing Rick's wheelchair into one of the many storage compartments lining the outside. Besides the three of us, six other passengers sat scattered across the gleaming greenish-blue seats that smelled of polished leather. Each seat had a small storage compartment underneath, perfect for our backpacks.

"How long's the ride?" Lindsey asked, breaking into a yawn.

Rick shrugged. "Depends on the stops. Maybe 2–3 hours."

"You can lean on me if you want to sleep, Lins," I said, offering her my shoulder.

Resting her head against me, she yawned again. "Thanks."

Minutes later, the motor came alive, and the doors swung shut. The bus hummed quietly as it started its maneuver toward the exit, then gained momentum as it turned onto the street. As I watched Los Angeles vanish into the darkness, I bounced my feet against the floor and swallowed a lump building inside my throat. My journey toward Bloodthirst and Margarete had begun.

CHAPTER 11

Castle Beach terminal next right," the bus driver announced over the loud speaker.

As the sign for Castle Beach rushed past the window, a slew of goose bumps rushed over my arms. My gaze cut to Rick. "I can't believe I'm really doing this."

He pointed a determined finger at me. "We're gonna find Margarete and fix this."

The bus veered right, slowing its pace as it hugged the off-ramp. Two lights up on the right illuminated the bus terminal, stretching out the length of a block. As we pulled into the entrance, a couple of speed bumps sent the bus swaying side to side and waking Lindsey. She pushed away from me, stretching her arms over her head and sighing. "We're here already?"

"Uh, yeah, three hours later," I corrected.

She blinked, then showed the whites of her eyes. "I slept the whole way?"

"That you did," Rick chimed in, before getting straight to the point. "I say we unload at the hotel, and then take a stroll and check out Bloodthirst. Probably closed, but you never know."

The bus driver looked over his shoulder at us. "This is your stop, kids."

Rick gave a nod to the bus driver. "Can you please get my wheelchair ready?"

"You got it," he answered before heading outside.

I scooted between Rick and Lindsey, gathered up our backpacks and handed them off. "C'mon, guys, we gotta go."

Lindsey's expression softened. "You nervous?"

"Of course, he is," Rick answered. "Hell, I'm even nervous."

"I'm nervous too," Lindsey admitted in a small voice.

"Geez, thanks, guys. I feel even more screwed now."

"Like I said, we're gonna fix this," Rick said with conviction.

"Yeah," Lindsey echoed.

I ran a hand through my hair and shrugged. "I guess."

The bus driver popped his head through the door. "Got your wheelchair ready." His hulk-like arms scooped Rick up like a feather, then set him down in his wheelchair. "You kids enjoy your stay at Castle Beach."

I stared at him and cocked my head just a bit. *Enjoy* wasn't the best choice of words to describe our trip.

"Thank you, we will," Rick offered up a polite response, then faced the terminal. "Let's head inside and see if there's a map. Not sure how far away the hotel is from here. Maybe there's a bus route, or if it's close, we can take a cab."

Lindsey walked ahead a few steps and glanced back at us. "The air smells like wet sand."

I shrugged. "We're probably close to the beach."

Lindsey reached the doors first and pulled them open, making way for Rick.

Inside the lobby, a large woman sat behind a massive information booth. Dark glasses swallowed up her face. She greeted us with one of those fake, cheery grins. "What can I do for ya?"

Rick wheeled closer to the counter. "Are the buses still running? Specifically, one that will take us to Haven Avenue?"

She chuckled and her whole body shook. "Son, buses don't go down to Haven Avenue after sunset." She let her glasses slide downward as she eyed the three of us. "Decent looking kids like yourselves have no business down on Haven."

"It's research for our school newspaper," Rick rattled off.

"Hmph." She sized us up once more before the phony smile returned. "Only transportation you can get right now is a cab. Would you like me to call one for you, honey?"

"Yes, that would be great," Rick replied. "Thank you."

"You got it." She pointed toward the entrance. "The cab will pull up just outside the front doors. Do be careful, now. It's a creepy neighborhood."

Rick acknowledged her with a polite nod. "We will. Thanks."

We claimed an empty bench by the front door, a perfect spot to keep watch for the cab. I sucked in a breath of nerves. This was it. Bloodthirst was in my grasp and maybe some much-needed answers.

Not even 10 minutes passed before a bright orange cab skidded into view. Rick blasted through the front door and was lengths ahead before Lindsey and I caught up with him. The cab driver packed Rick's wheelchair into the truck as we settled into the back seat.

"Where to?"

"1105 Haven Avenue," Rick offered up.

The driver recklessly screeched away from the building, throwing us back against the seat yet again as he cruised down the street, humming out loud.

"Vampires are nothing compared to this guy's driving," I whispered.

Lindsey clamped a palm over her mouth and stifled a giggle.

Rick smirked. "We'll be fine."

Even with the lightning bolt speed, it seemed like forever before he came to an abrupt stop in front of Sleeptime Lodge. As Rick paid the fare, I peered at the two-story cream building with red-brick pillars.

Lindsey sighed. "Thank God, it's not a dump."

How it looked meant nothing to me. I wasn't there for the room. I had one goal, and one goal only, to rid myself of this thing.

"I'll check in and get the keys."

I pulled the hotel door open for Rick. "Do you need any money?"

He waved me away. "Nah, I got it."

"Okay, well, just let us know when you do." I noticed the elevator just left of the front desk. "We'll wait by the elevator." Rick acknowledged me with a nod.

Lindsey and I reached the elevator just as Rick got the keys, so I punched the call button.

The elevator chimed as Rick called out, "We've got rooms 9 and 10."

Being 3 a.m., we were the only ones taking the ride up. We vacated the elevator in single file and spread out in the hallway, scanning door numbers. Our rooms stood at the end of the hall on opposite sides.

Rick popped the lock on his room. "Let's unload and head to the club."

Lindsey gave an enthusiastic thumbs-up. "For sure."

The unknown prickled my flesh with goose bumps. I wasn't sure how I felt about it. I guess I should've been as eager as Rick and Lindsey, but none of us knew what Bloodthirst would bring. Regardless, I agreed. "I'm in."

The hotel room was nothing special, with two full size beds, covered in colorful plaid bedspreads. A dresser stood between the two beds, and a writing desk with a TV overhead claimed the opposite wall. A small refrigerator stuck in the corner of the room looked like an afterthought. We threw our packs on the bed and headed toward the door. Lindsey charged back to the bed to slip a stake inside her hoodie.

I busted out laughing. "C'mon, you can see the tip sticking out."

She shoved it deeper into her pocket. "I'm not going without protection."

I waved her away. "Whatever, let's just go."

"I'll bet Rick brings one too."

"You're probably right," I agreed, pushing her out the door.

Rick sat waiting by the elevator with a map spread out in his lap and a stake peeking out of his pocket.

Lindsey showed off hers. "Got mine right here."

He grinned. "We're prepared."

I opened my mouth to criticize, then stopped short. No use wasting my breath on the Van Helsing twins.

The hum of the elevator announced its approach, and once again we had it to ourselves. The hotel lobby looked like a scene straight out of a zombie apocalypse movie; dead quiet and vacant. We were the only crazies running around at 3 a.m., but outside the hotel, a few shady looking characters passed us by.

Rick tapped a spot on the map, then pointed up the street. "According to the map, Bloodthirst is about two and half blocks from the hotel."

I followed his finger, squinting as I surveyed the street. Normalcy stared back. I heaved a sigh. "Not what I'd expected to see, and kind of a letdown." I pressed forward, shoving my hands in my pockets.

"There," Lindsey blurted out, pointing up the street and sprinting in the direction of her finger. "That red glow's gotta be it."

I broke out into a jog while Rick whooshed past both of us. The pitch-black building with its gleaming gold door and "Bloodthirst" in brilliant red neon letters floating over the entrance, brought us skidding to a stop.

"This is so cool." Lindsey's gaze bounced all over the building, like she didn't know where to look first. "Like it came right out of a horror movie."

"There's a keypad on the side of the door," Rick said, rolling closer. "Did the person from the chatroom give you any kind of code?"

"Code? No. All they said was to ask for Margarete."

"Maybe we should knock," Lindsey offered up.

Rick shrugged. "Can't hurt."

I approached the elaborate gold door, and a thick wall of salty-sweet copper slammed into my brain, knocking me backward. My pulse climbed sharply as cold shivers erupted down my spine. I bolted into the street, panting out gusts of air. As distance grew between me and Bloodthirst, the sensation weakened.

Lindsey rushed to my side, shouting, "What is it? What's wrong?"

"There's blood." I took a breath. "A ton of it." Another breath. "Behind that door."

Lindsey set her sights on the door. "Then I'll knock."

I held her back. "Let Rick."

"I'll do it." He said, already halfway to the door. He pounded hard. No one came. He hammered the door a second and third time. Still nothing. "They're in there. Why aren't they answering?" He glanced over his shoulder. "I think we need a code."

I stepped back onto the sidewalk with Lindsey glued to my side, shaking my head. "I told you, I didn't get any code. Looks like we'll just have to come back tomorrow."

As if the door had ears, it slowly swung open, releasing a whoosh of cool air. A tall, lanky man, with snow-white skin, appeared in the doorway. He aimed a serious scowl at Rick and growled out a, "Yes?"

Rick sighed with relief, oblivious to the man's exasperation. "Finally. We're here to see Margarete."

"No one enters after the events have started." He waved us away. "Come back tomorrow."

I charged forward, then shoved my foot in the doorway before it closed. "Les Vampires sent me here." His expression remained unchanged.

"They could go by Bloodletting," I added with a shrug.

He crossed his arms over his chest. "Reciting names you found off the internet will not grant you access."

"What about Hypatia? Does that name do anything for ya?"

The words had scarcely left my lips when he gripped my neck and shoved me against the building, his cold breath stinging my face. "Tell me how you know of this name!"

Lindsey shrieked, "Brandon," as she dashed forward.

Rick latched onto her. "Lindsey, no!"

As he stared me down with his intense, crystal-blue orbs my heartbeat exploded, booming inside my chest. I'd hit a nerve. Obviously, Hypatia had meant something to him or he knew of her, but he sure as hell didn't look like he was going to tell me. I had to use his reaction to my advantage. I had to outsmart him. I threw my own uncompromising expression at him as I said, "I'll only tell Margarete."

His lips curled, revealing long, deadly fangs coated with sticky saliva. I flinched. *Oh God, he's gonna bite me.* Instead, he just dropped me and stormed back into the club. Lindsey dashed to my side. Flinging her arms around my neck, she started bawling. Rick parked his chair inches from me, gripping my hand. "I'm okay. It's okay," I assured them.

Once again, the door opened. A tall, skinny girl appeared, sweeping her long raven hair off her shoulders. I shoved Lindsey behind me as Rick used his wheelchair as a barricade, shielding us. Her sheer, violet-colored eyes lit up, then she smirked, exposing razor-sharp fangs. "Aw, members of the Scooby Doo gang have come to visit."

I stepped in front of Rick, then cocked my head. "You're Margarete?"

Her gaze narrowed as she focused her attention on me. "That I am."

"I'm Brandon. This is Lindsey, and this is Rick."

She vanished, then reappeared in front of me, so close our noses touched. A dark haze altered the violet hue of her eyes as she peered into mine. My hands, arms, then whole body shook uncontrollably, but I couldn't look away from her.

"Strange," she let slip, then sniffed the base of my neck.

Again, my heartbeat slammed into my rib cage, but I kept my mouth shut, certain she'd bite me if I spoke.

She inhaled deeper, lacing my throat with her icy breath. Abruptly, she pushed away, a gasp fleeing her lips. "How can this be? You are mortal, yet a vampire's soul exists inside you."

Margarete confirmed Eve's reading, Rick's research, my research, the blood cravings...and everything I'd done, turning the nightmare into reality. I fell against Lindsey, releasing an uncontrollable sob as her arms came around me.

"Do you know Hypatia?" Rick asked, taking charge.

"Of course," Margarete boasted.

"We think she may be at the center of all this. Brandon was told you could contact her."

Margarete tilted her head and pursed her lips as if she were mulling over her response. "You've intrigued me." She gave a sharp nod. "Yes, I will contact her; however, whether she accepts my invitation is up to her. Come back tomorrow, and we will see if she shows. The club is quite popular, and it has rules. You must arrive before sunset if you want to get in." She turned her lips into a brokenhearted pout. "And it would be a shame if you were to miss her."

"That's not gonna happen. I won't miss her."

Rick waved me down. "We'll be sure to get here on time."

CHAPTER 12

As Margarete instructed, we arrived at Bloodthirst just before sunset, only to discover a line of people spilling out into the street, with their gazes glued to the black and gold door. I heaved a sigh that rattled my lips, then threw my hand in their direction. "It's like a *Star Wars* premiere. What if we don't get in?"

Rick rolled up next to me and gripped my shoulder. "We'll get in."

The woman ahead of us turned, flashed a toothy smile, and said, "Don't be nervous. I come here a lot." She pointed down the line of people. "It's when the line reaches the end of the block that they turn people away." Her brownish-green eyes looked me up and down. "There are always more humans than vampires, so if you want to be chosen, you have to stand out."

Chosen? Chosen for what? "What do you mean, chosen?"

She giggled that "I know something you don't" tune before a serious expression inched its way across her face. "You'll find out when you get inside."

Someone screamed, "They're letting us in!" and my heart jumped into my throat.

"Good luck," the woman mumbled, then turned and rushed forward.

Rick scratched his head. "Good luck? Odd comment."

"If you ask me," Lindsey whispered, "she was just plain weird."

Her good luck comment evaporated all the saliva in my mouth, but considering my circumstances, it seemed appropriate. "I'm nervous about the blood. What if I freak out or something when we're inside? What if I can't control myself or you can't control me?"

"We stick to the plan, find Hypatia, then get out," Rick recapped. "You'll be okay."

I gave a quick nod, and Lindsey did too, but I had no clue what would happen once we got inside.

The entrance grew closer and so did the faint smell of stale blood. It drifted right under my nose, and I darted my tongue over my lips, shivering. Tonight, I had to stay in control and not let the power influence my actions, especially in the presence of blood. *Go away!* I shouted inside my head, holding my breath and shutting out the scent. My muscles relaxed as a sense of self-control flooded through my veins. I exhaled, as it appeared I'd regained control, but for how long was up to the power.

The same man, or vampire, who refused to let us in the night before, herded the crowd through the door like sheep. A few steps in, the temperature took a nosedive, and I choked on the freezing air. Several gasps later, I zipped my jacket up to my neck and pulled Lindsey close to my side. Her pulse thumped against my body like Morse code.

"Keep moving," the pale man called out, shooing us forward.

Like zombies, we shuffled along the dark red walls and into the heart of the dimly lit club. Everyone gathered around a raised stage in the center. A bunch of circular, black-velvet booths seemed to be the only seating, and in the very back, I could make out two bars spreading the length of the club walls.

Everyone started clapping and pushing forward, drawing my attention to the stage. A man with gleaming, turquoise-colored eyes stood centerstage, spreading his arms wide. "Welcome." His voice came across like eerie music that grabs your attention instantly. "The doors to Bloodthirst are now locked."

I skimmed the crowd, their dreamy expressions fixated on him, like he was a rock star or something. Did I miss something? I squinted hard at him. Nope, nothing there, just some guy with intense eyes.

"The club has a few simple rules," he continued. "Vampires are free to come and go as they please. Humans may exit Bloodthirst at any time; however, once you vacate the premises, you will not be allowed to reenter. If a vampire approaches you, you may choose either to accept or refuse their kiss. If you refuse, the vampire must respect your wishes and walk away. We will guarantee your safety." His ruby lips rose into a devilish grin. "If you accept, you do so at your own risk, so please, choose wisely." He waved his hand in the air. "Let the events begin."

People bolted in every direction, infected with hookup syndrome. Lip-locks of the blood persuasion kind exploded on all sides, scenting the air with salty human gore. I inhaled a breath, then another and another, flooding my body with feverish hunger. With every ounce of strength, I dug my fingernails into my clenched fists and shoved the blood cravings back down my throat.

Lindsey's eyes bulged from their sockets, and her mouth hung slack. She snapped it shut, then blinked several times. "That's fake, right?"

"Jesus," Rick breathed. "I think it's real."

Over the gasping and moaning, I shouted out, "Stick to the plan. Remember, our sole purpose is to find Hypatia."

Rick gripped the wheels of his chair and jerked away from the stage. "You're right. Keep your eyes peeled for Margarete."

I pulled a dazed Lindsey back and kept her close as we zigzagged between a row of humans dropping like flies from a vampire's embrace. A clear identifier was the brilliance of their haunting, hypnotizing, jewel-like eyes, and since death was not our destiny, I kept mine lowered and a hand over Lindsey's.

Rick shouted over the chaos, "She's at the bar." Then aimed his wheelchair straight for her, clearing a path.

As I stood behind Margarete, staring at her raven hair glistening under bar lights, my stomach twisted in knots. What if she had no news about Hypatia? What if Hypatia didn't show? What then? Had I come all this way for nothing? I'd never know if I didn't make myself known. I softly tapped Margarete's shoulder.

She turned with an unhurried pace and faced me, then hooked her arm around the auburn-haired man with pale flesh standing next to her. She bobbed her head in my direction. "Caleb, this is the boy, Brandon, I was telling you about."

His diamond-like hazel eyes centered on me, then jumped to Lindsey. His scarlet lips flashed into a wicked grin. "But you failed tell me about this gorgeous gem filled with virgin blood." He narrowed the gap between himself and Lindsey.

"And who might you be?"

Lindsey's large green eyes fixated on him as she whispered, "His sister."

Okay, so he wasn't a man, but a vampire. At once, I threw myself in front of him, blocking his path and guarding Lindsey.

"Leave her alone."

Margarete tossed her hair over her shoulder, then pointed a finger in Caleb's face. "And your ticket into the doghouse if you so much as harm a hair on her pretty little head."

A sinister laugh flowed from Caleb's mouth before he kissed Margarete's cheek. "Kidding, love." He rubbed his stomach and added, "Besides, already had my fill."

Margarete leveled her violet orbs at him before shifting them on me. She gestured toward an empty booth across from the bar with a bottle of wine and five glasses. "Let us sit and share some wine."

Like we had a choice. Doing as she requested, we slid into the booth. Rick parked his chair next to Lindsey, and I sandwiched her in on the other side, leaving no chance for this Caleb character to make a move on her. Margarete filled glasses with wine and passed them around the table. "Drink." Rick gulped his down in one swallow.

I pushed Lindsey's away, as well as my own. "We're not old enough."

Soft laughter spilled from her mouth. Smiling wide, she exposed her razor-sharp fangs. "There is no age limit here. Go ahead."

Lindsey reached for hers and took a small sip, then grimaced. I refused altogether. I needed a clear head.

Margarete rested her hand on Caleb's arm as she gestured to me. "Look in his eyes and tell me what you see."

"Already took a peek." He took a sip of wine. "Awful crowded in that body of his."

"So, you sense the other?" Margarete pressed.

Caleb kept his mouth shut as he gazed into her eyes; maybe he didn't want to admit what he'd seen, or maybe it was more about admitting that Margarete had been right, but finally, he nodded. "I did."

A deep, gratifying sigh spilled from her lips before she planted them on his and kissed him. "I love it when you admit I'm right." She turned to me, and her mouth slowly turned downward. "I sent a mental message to Hypatia, informing her of your arrival. She has not responded, I'm afraid."

My heart thudded dully in my chest as her words sunk in. "I came all this way..." My voice cracked as I slumped forward.

Lindsey's arm came around me. "Don't give up."

Rick's voice projected over the crowd. "Then message her again!"

"If I thought it would help, I would."

That soft, sweet lullaby I knew so well rang inside my ears.

Lindsey grabbed my arm. "Do you hear that?" She jumped up onto the seat and stood on her tiptoes, her gaze darting about. "I know that voice, that lullaby. Oh my God, Brandon, it's the one from when we were kids!"

She was right, and the humming was coming from inside the club. I knew it was Hypatia and sprang onto the seat next to Lindsey, but there were too many humans and vampires fused together. "Hypatia!" I shouted, waving my arms overhead. "Over here."

"Good heavens," Margarete scolded as she yanked both Lindsey and I back down. "Monkeys leap about and act like fools, not humans. Behave!"

Caleb chuckled. "I found it rather amusing."

Rick scooted closer to the table and leaned in toward me. "What? Did you see something?"

"I heard this—"

"Lullaby," Lindsey rattled off. "Some ghost used to hum it all the time when we were kids."

Margarete locked her violet orbs on Lindsey. "Ghost?"

"Ghost?" Rick echoed.

A delicate scent of dried flowers and spices perfumed the air around us, then a female voice said, "Dear humans, I am much more than a ghost."

Lindsey jumped slightly, let out a gasp, then latched onto my arm. "It's her."

I whipped my head around so fast, a string of heat throbbed up my neck, but the pain simply vanished as I gazed into a pair of striking ocean-blue eyes staring down at me.

Margarete appeared next to her when a second ago, she sat across the table from me. "I see you got my message."

Caleb also moved with the speed of light, greeting the girl. "Always a pleasure."

She barely acknowledged them with a nod. I was her focus.

As I gazed at her, the power forced the chaos of Bloodthirst to fade into the background; only she mattered, and I had to get closer, close enough to touch her. I hugged her, pressing my chest against hers, feeling our hearts pound on top each other.

Blood tears moistened her eyes, then she quickly wiped them away. "At last, we meet."

Rick wedged his wheelchair between us, separating us, demanding, "Tell us who you are."

She bent down to his eye level. "Look me in the eyes and tell me you don't know who I am?"

He held his ground. "I need you to say it."

She cocked her head of chocolate-brown hair, wrinkled her prefect brow, and disregarded him with a wave of her hand. Something pulled her gaze back to Rick, then she winked before stabbing a fang into her finger. "A handsome face deserves to be handsome."

He leaned backward, putting distance between them.

"Really, it doesn't bother—"

"Hush!" she ordered, then smeared her blood around his marred face.

Every scar rippled, stretched taut, then flattened into perfectly smooth skin. I blinked, did a double take, then choked on a mouthful of air. His face looked flawless, and hair was growing in the bald spots!

She stepped back and regarded her handiwork. "Much better."

"Oh my God, Rick!" Lindsey shouted.

Rick's hands flew to his face, brushing them over the surface. He gasped out loud. "I can't feel my scars. Are they gone?"

I grabbed his hand and squeezed it. "Yes!"

He stroked his smooth face as he gazed at the vampire that healed him. His mouth opened several times, but no words came out.

Watching her control Rick with her blood made me realize how desperately I wanted my freedom. I faced her jewel-like orbs that mimicked the sea and said exactly who she was. "You're Hypatia, a vampire, and linked to the one inside me that I'm going to rid myself of."

Her cherry red lips spread into a bemused smile. "Correct, but you're sadly mistaken if you think you can just walk away. Your sole purpose is to become my companion."

An internal force tugged at my core, thrusting me an inch closer to Hypatia. I dug my heels into the ground and fought the magnetic pull with all my might. "You wish."

Lindsey latched onto my arms and yanked backward. "You can't have my brother."

Rick sat motionless, staring off in the distance, with his hand plastered to his face.

Caleb flashed in front of Hypatia. "Hang on now, blue eyes. Forcing a turn is not our bag."

Hypatia's hand slightly trembled as she threw a piercing scowl Caleb's way. "This is none of your concern."

He took his eyes off Hypatia and glanced back at me. "How old are you?"

The sudden awareness of my birthday spread a warm flush over my skin. Hanging out in a vampire club, arguing my faith wasn't exactly how I thought I'd spend it. "I'll be 17 tomorrow."

He spun around and blurted out, "Seriously?"

"It's true," Lindsey confirmed.

Hypatia seemed less affected. "That changes nothing."

Caleb wiggled a finger at her. "Oh, but it does. The lad's only 17. We have rules, crafted by your own brother and my maker."

She crossed her arms and huffed in his face. "To every rule there is an exception."

He smirked. "This one's not your call, and you know it."

Their rule was gibberish. They should've included one about robbing a human of their body. "I just want my life back."

"And I want my brother back," Lindsey added in a shrill voice.

Rick finally shook off his daze and spoke up. "Besides, why turn someone who'd only resent you for it?"

Hypatia fluttered her long, thick eyelashes at him. "Do *you* resent my taking away your scars?"

Rick touched his face once more, then blushed. "That was a very kind gesture, but Brandon's a teenager. His whole life is ahead of him—a human life. Why not give him that and walk away?"

Caleb slapped Rick on the back. "Well said!"

Hypatia rolled her eyes at them, then waved them away like she couldn't be bothered with such nonsense.

I clamped my hands over my ears, wishing everyone would shut up. There was only one agenda here, and that was ridding myself of this damn creature. That should be every-one's focus, not rules or turning. My arms grew rigid, the tension running into my fingers, curling them into fists. "You can't have my life!" I shouted. "Whatever you did to get this thing inside, you need to reverse it and get it out!"

Hypatia's eyelids narrowed into slits, shooting daggers at me. "There is no getting *it* out. You must become one with the vampire within."

My heart seemed to freeze, then pound as I defied her. "That's not gonna happen!"

Lindsey charged toward Hypatia, but Rick jerked her back. "Lindsey, don't."

She yanked free, fluttering her hands and shouting, "Someone, help us, please!"

Lindsey was right, things had spiraled out of control. Hypatia came to satisfy her own needs, and so had I. Were my expectations unreasonable? Was my only choice to sacrifice myself over to the power? If I tried to restrain the power, it'd only take control like it had, but I couldn't just give myself over to it either. I had to fight. "There's got to be another way to fix this. Because this"—I gestured to my whole body—"is not happening."

Margarete whispered something into Caleb's ear.

He raised his eyebrows, then kissed her cheek. "Brilliant, love." He set his sights on Hypatia. "I see a journey to The Council in our future."

Hypatia clutched at the locket around her neck as a visible shiver ran through her. "I will not stand before my brother. His judgement will be less than fair."

Caleb placed his hand over his heart as he said, "I will ensure Kohath remains impartial."

Her eyes centered on him and narrowed. "You would do this for me, why?"

Margarete stepped forward and took Hypatia's hands. "Because it is the right thing to do. I will accompany Caleb to ensure he keeps his word."

He eyed his companion with a slackened mouth. "When have I ever...strike that." He spread his arms wide and blew Margarete a kiss. "I wouldn't have it any other way."

Again, they kept us in the dark. I tapped Margarete on the shoulder. "Mind telling us what the plan is?"

Before she could answer, Hypatia blurted out, "They want us to stand before The Council and plead our case."

Rick cocked his head, studying Hypatia. "Like a court trial?" He bobbed his head toward Caleb. "As he pointed out, you have rules, so why address a council?"

"We have a boy," Caleb said, wagging a finger at me, "housing an ancient vampire's soul. On the other hand,"—he spun around and presented Hypatia with a wave of his hand—"we have a lovesick Old One—for you human folk, that's a very old vampire—who wants to reunite with her lover stuck inside this boy. Neither party agrees; therefore, we are at an impasse." He paused and took stock of our expressions. "You follow?" He didn't wait for a reply and continued. "The Council, one of 12 wise vampires, will hear both sides and determine the appropriate verdict."

"What case? I'm the victim here. I didn't consent to any of this crap." I pointed at Hypatia. "She's in the wrong, not me."

Hypatia gave a flippant shrug of her shoulders. "I'll get what I want eventually. The vampire within you will grow too powerful to contain. Then you'll be mine."

Her words slithered into my stomach, and I trembled. I was human, incapable of conquering something as powerful as a vampire. Hypatia certainly wasn't going to help me. Maybe pleading my case to this council was my way out. Maybe they had means to drive the power from my body.

"How do I get in front of this council?"

Hypatia drew her mouth into a straight line, then glared at Margarete and Caleb. "Your bright idea, you explain."

A noticeable breath escaped Margarete's lips before she turned away from Hypatia to face me. "You must travel to their haven in Scotland."

Her words spun around my head, then I blinked. "What did you just say?"

Lindsey smacked my arm. "Omg! She said Scotland."

"Um, the country?"

Caleb winked and began cackling. "Yes, country."

Rick was quick to point out, "We don't have the means to fly to Scotland."

"Naïve mortals," Caleb mumbled. "Vampire airways at your service."

My gaze darted back and forth between the three pairs of jewel-like orbs peering at us. I cut my hand through the air. "No way."

Lindsey bounced on her toes, and her eyes lit up. "Yes way. C'mon, Brandon!"

I grabbed her by the shoulders and forced her still. "What if they dropped us? No, it's too dangerous."

Caleb burst out laughing. "Ha! Absurd."

Margarete playfully nudged him away. "Behave." Her expression softened as she faced me. "You will be perfectly safe. I promise."

Rick huffed, patting the side of his chair. "Hello, wheelchair here."

Hypatia glided over to him like a ballerina. "I find your"—she circled her hand over his legs, then face—"quirks interesting, a challenge if you will. I will fly you." She scowled at his wheelchair. "But that contraption stays here."

He barked out a laugh. "Then how do you suppose I get around?"

"Leave that to me," she answered, then faced Caleb and Margarete. "Choose the boy or the girl as your flight companion so we may leave."

I compressed my lips, biting into them as I watched the self-absorbed vampire strut around, blasting out orders. She seemed to be the mastermind behind this whole mess with one agenda in mind, resurrecting the creature inside of me. Maybe the power never had a choice. It did seem to relinquish control as soon as she showed up. Well, I was standing firm. I got up in her personal space. "You know my name; use it! You don't give a shit that you screwed up my life—my family's. All you care about is yourself. Maybe that's why you're alone."

A dark storm brewed behind Hypatia's eyes as she locked them on me. She placed her lips inches from mine and hissed, "What I *care* about is my dead lover's soul inside you." She took a step back, then looked me up and down. "You, on the other hand, are of no importance to me."

"That's not true," Lindsey challenged. "I was there, remember? Every time Brandon cried, pouted, felt sorry for himself, whatever, you came and hummed that creepy lullaby."

I stared at my sister, feeling a lump swell in my throat, but Hypatia waved her away like a pesky little bug.

Lindsey latched onto Hypatia's arm and forced her to listen. "I'm not gonna shut up, and you know what I'm talking about. You like Brandon a lot. You're acting all tough 'cause you're scared something might go wrong and Brandon may get hurt."

Lins always had my back, but a perceptive Lindsey? I kind of liked it. I gave her a fist pump before looking back to Hypatia.

A slight tremble gripped Hypatia's chin, then it was gone. "How dare you presume to understand my emotions," she spewed. "I've walked this earth for centuries, and you're a mere human and a child."

Lindsey held her ground, standing up to Hypatia. "Correction, teenager, and I know when someone likes my brother."

A blood-red film spread over Hypatia's eyes, spilling into the corners. She let out a whimper then bolted, vanishing into the crowd. A gush of air brushed against my cheek as Caleb, then Margarete, blasted off after her.

Rick sat stiffly, staring at the empty space. "What the hell just happened? So, do we go after them?"

"Let's go after them," Lindsey parroted.

Chasing after Hypatia would send the wrong message. "She'll come back. I've got what she wants."

"Good thinking," Rick agreed. "That'll show you can't be manipulated."

No sooner had the words left his mouth, Caleb and Margarete appeared with Hypatia sandwiched between them. Hypatia tossed a brief look my way. "I have been insensitive, and for that I apologize."

I couldn't tell if her apology was sincere or forced, but I gave her a nod of acknowledgment and said, "Thank you."

"We should get going if we want to beat the sun," Margarete pointed out.

Caleb grinned and rubbed his hands together. "Ooh, I love a good game of cat and mouse."

"Not with humans in our arms," Margarete scolded.

He seemed oblivious to Margarete's warning, as his focus was on Lindsey. He flashed my sister a wicked smirk. "I'll fly the gem."

Margarete yanked Lindsey away from Caleb and shoved me in front of him. "You get Brandon."

Caleb's smile slipped into a sneer. "Marvelous."

I echoed the sentiment. "You're not my first choice either." Chuckling, he slapped me on the back.

"What about my wheelchair?" Rick questioned a second time, glancing at Hypatia.

Hypatia's reply was an exaggerated sigh before she turned away.

Margarete rolled her eyes at her before facing Rick. "We'll store it in the back, in the crematorium."

A pale color washed over Rick's face, and he swallowed hard. "Wonderful."

I shrugged. "What's a crematorium?"

Margarete arched her brow, then pursed her lips as if conjuring up the right words. "A furnace where we cremate the corpses," she revealed with candor, then added, "Of course, after they've been kissed."

Lindsey scrunched up her face like she'd eaten something nasty. "Gross."

I imagined charred bodies piled on top of each other, vaporizing into a rancid stench. I looked Margarete in the eyes and accused, "In other words, you burn them?"

"What else would you have us do with them? Stack them up around the club? The smell would be horrendous."

What a callous response. Were we just a bunch of worthless creatures? "But they're people," I pointed out. "Someone's brother or sister, or parent. Doesn't that mean anything to you?"

"Look around you. Do you see fine dining, a DJ, a band, dancing?" she mocked. "No, you see hunger, nothing more, nothing less."

"And people die," I added.

"But they're warned each night."

Caleb pushed us apart. "Enough chitchat. If this little journey is happening tonight, then liftoff is in T-minus 10."

"It must be tonight!" Hypatia's voice gushed with urgency.

Margarete acknowledged Hypatia with a firm nod, then glanced toward the bar and snapped her fingers. "Darius, come here."

A male dressed in black and covered in tattoos appeared at her side. "Yes, Margarete."

"We need to take a little trip," she explained. "Stash this wheelchair in the back until we return."

He grinned, revealing bloodstained fangs. "Of course." In the next second, he snatched it out from underneath Rick.

Rick's arms flailed about as his legs crumpled beneath him, but Hypatia scooped him up before he hit the ground. Sneering at the tattooed vamp, she spat, "You could have warned us."

He blew Hypatia a kiss, snickered, then hoisted Rick's wheelchair overhead and vanished.

"Thank you," Rick said, wrapping an arm around Hypatia's neck.

She flashed an inviting smile on her cherry red lips. "For you, anytime."

"Good Lord," Caleb groaned before winking at Margarete. "Ready?"

She nodded, plastering a hefty frown on her flawless forehead. "We travel at great speeds. You *will* lose consciousness, but our blood will ensure your safety."

Lindsey inched closer to me, and the weight of responsibility sat on my shoulders. I looked to Margarete. "Um...what do you mean by your blood?"

"You must drink a few drops of our blood; otherwise, you will not regain consciousness."

"Whoa, wait a minute! I can't ask my sister to drink vampire blood."

"There's no other way," Margarete flatly stated.

My gaze drifted toward Lindsey and Rick. Lindsey gagged, and Rick plastered a "what the" expression on his face. "Rick, take Lindsey home. I can't ask either of you to do this."

Lindsey punched my arm. "Are you serious? I'm not leaving you with a bunch of vampires. No way."

Rick gave a curt nod. "I'm not going anywhere, man."

"So, it's settled," Margarete concluded. Spearing her finger, she squeezed out a small dot of blood and offered it to Lindsey.

Lindsey opened her mouth, and Caleb swooped in. Before I could push him out of the way, he deposited a few drops of his own blood into Lindsey's mouth. She forced it down with a shiver. "Yuck!"

Caleb winked at Margarete, then flashed her his pearly whites. "Sorry, love."

Margarete's violet orbs narrowed to slits. She tossed an icy glare at Caleb and growled out, "You're such an ass."

I looked back and forth between them and shouted, "But what does it mean?"

Margarete grabbed me by the shoulders. "Calm down, it means nothing." She scowled at Caleb once more. "He loves pushing my buttons, that's all."

"So, he can't, like, control her or something?"

"What?" Lindsey blurted out.

Caleb huffed. "Just razzing Margarete. Don't you people know how to have fun?"

Hypatia, with Rick in her arms, interjected. "Stop it, all of you! Brandon, your sister is fine. I've given Rick my blood." She pressed on her pierced finger, drawing out more blood. "Your turn."

As her finger neared my mouth, a familiar scent of rust and metal drifted under my nose, and not because I'd tasted human blood. This was different. I jerked my head upward, locking my gaze on her. The ocean-blue color of her eyes darkened as she acknowledged me with a curt nod. "I'll explain later. Now, drink."

I obeyed and opened my mouth. Several salty drops landed on my tongue, and I could've sworn I'd just swallowed my own blood.

"Come," Margarete said, ushering us toward the club's entrance.

Hypatia cleared a path, steering us toward the front door. The second my foot hit the sidewalk, I sucked in a breath of fresh air, ridding my lungs of the blood and death of Bloodthirst. I hadn't even exhaled as a blast of wind whooshed through my hair, then Rick's screech pierced my eardrum, followed by Lindsey's. My skin tingled as I whirled around, scanning the street. There was only me and Caleb. He erased the distance between us, then smirked. "Up, up, and away," he chuckled.

CHAPTER 13

The next time I opened my eyes, I sat slumped in some throne-like chair, facing a bunch of people stuck in a time warp. As the fog cleared my head, I bolted upright, searching for Lindsey. She claimed a chair to my left, and Rick was on her right, sitting in someone's wheelchair, both shaking off the daze and coming to. I reached out and touched Lindsey's arm. "Are you okay?"

She swept her hair off her face and tucked it behind her ears, then slowly nodded. "I think so."

I glanced down at Rick. "You okay?"

"Yeah. You?"

"I'm good." My gaze double backed to the bizarre people decked out in flowy gowns. One male with super blonde hair was in a secret huddle with Hypatia, Margarete, and Caleb. The others started to gather around a long marble table in the center of the bare room.

The blonde male suddenly took notice of us and broke free from the discussion. "I see our visitors have awakened." He gestured toward a tray of bottled water in the center of the table. "May I offer you some water, perhaps?"

"I would love some water," Rick answered with a raise of his hand. As his hand landed on the arm of the chair, he snapped his head upright. "Whose wheelchair is this?"

Hypatia grabbed a bottle and appeared at his side. "Your water." She rested her hand on the back of the wheelchair. "I had my brother locate one for you."

Rick turned all kinds of red, then cleared his throat. "Thank you."

"Let us make our introductions," The blonde male said, taking control of the conversation and placing his hand on his chest. "I am Kohath, Head of The Council, Hypatia's brother and maker." The sheen of his olive-colored eyes brightened as he gripped Caleb's shoulder in a fatherly way. "I am also Caleb's maker." He gestured toward the others around the table. "These are members of our council."

Margarete stepped behind our chairs and introduced us. "This is Brandon. Next to him is his sister, Lindsey, and finally, we have their friend, Rick."

The one named Kohath dipped his chin at her. "Thank you, Margarete."

Hypatia whisked past Margarete and over to me. "This is the boy I have spoken of." She pointed a firm finger at each council member. "Come witness the truth behind his eyes, then bow at my feet and beg for my forgiveness."

Kohath motioned the others to remain seated, then turned to Hypatia. "I will be the one to observe this boy."

"Then I challenge you, dear brother, to deny what you see."

With a slow, steady gait, he approached me. As he peered into my eyes, a slight tremor shook his shoulders. His gaze darted to Hypatia. "How is this so? What have you done?"

She chose the middle of the room, drawing attention to herself. "I have a story to tell."

Kohath arched his thick pale brows and cautioned,

"Hypatia, do not waste The Council's time with fairy tales."

She waved him away with a flick of her wrist. "As I said, I have a story to tell."

Kohath pursed his lips and let out a groan.

"Dude, don't waste your breath," I offered. "I have a sister, I know. They do what they want."

Simultaneously, Lindsey and Hypatia hushed me.

I gave Kohath the palm gesture. "Need I say more?"

He acknowledged my sarcasm with a slight nod, then turned his attention to his sister. "You have the floor, Hypatia."

She held her chin high as she walked the length of the table, eyeing The Council. "My tragedy is common knowledge among you. The only man I'd loved, the only man I'd turned, killed by my own father." Her forehead drew tight, tugging at her brows. She gritted her teeth as if fighting off a downpour of sobs. "True love never dies; it finds its way back home."

I flinched and gripped the chair arms, feeling her pain as my own, but I barely knew her. My heart wasn't invested.

This was the power's agony flowing through my veins.

Hypatia paused, wrestling to hold her quivering chin still before her superior nature resurfaced, squashing any sign of emotion. "Lucius *did* come back to me. I witnessed his soul struggling to survive as it passed from mortal to mortal."

What? Wait a minute. There were others? I scanned The Council's stone expressions, not a blink, flinch, or twitch in response, but Lindsey, Rick, and I sure as hell took notice. "How many times did I plead for help?" Hypatia fired off, redirecting my attention. A crazed look marred her beautiful face as she scolded The Council. "You judged me, accused me of madness." She thrust a hand my way. "There sits my proof, and Kohath, your leader, witnessed Lucius inside the boy."

Why did she keep referring to me as "the boy?" She damn well knew my name. Was Lindsey right? Was Hypatia worried about my safety? Was disassociating my name to my face a coping mechanism? As I considered it, Hypatia passed in front of me, leveling a scorching gaze on The Council. Nope, definitely not the reason.

"It is time to reveal what I've kept hidden all these years." Hypatia paused, spreading her lips into a taunting grin. "Why Lucius's soul was able to survive within Brandon and not the others."

There it was! She said my name! I jumped to my feet and thrust my fist into the air. "Yes!" Why I needed her to recognize me as a person, I had no clue, but it felt awesome.

Lindsey smothered a bark of laughter into her palm, and Rick gave me a thumbs-up, but The Council's scowls said otherwise. Kohath arched his thick brows at me, waving me back down.

I rattled off a quick, "I'm sorry," as I reclaimed my seat.

Hypatia flashed a pleased look my way before resuming her tale. "I am a vampire of many years and many powers. One night, long ago, a whisper of blood led me to an evil man digging through a very pregnant women's purse while she lay limp. The blood I tracked was hers, bleeding from the knife he'd buried in her chest." She gestured toward Lindsey and me. "This woman was your mother, and although she has no recollection of the incident, I saved her life and the life of her unborn child—you, Brandon."

I edged off my seat, but Kohath's disapproving glare and raised hand shut me down. Lindsey, on the other hand, whipped her head toward Hypatia and challenged, "My mom would've remembered something like that, told us even."

"I erased it from her memory," Hypatia explained. "What human witnesses their own murder, their killer's execution, and their own revival all at the hands of a vampire? Had I not cleared it from her mind, she would have gone mad."

Hypatia's statement drew a whimper from Lindsey. I reached for my sister's hand as my own sorrow tickled my throat. Hypatia had nothing to gain from making up such a scene, but why erase this memory and not the one from the hospital?

"I terminated the wretched man's life," Hypatia said through gritted teeth. "I tossed him aside and quickly tended to your mother. The wound was too deep. Distress pulsated in the baby's—Brandon's—heart. Its tiny thump echoed inside my ears. To save her," Hypatia said, and paused, looking directly at me, "and you, I sliced open my wrist and poured my blood into her mouth, forcing her to drink. As she drank, I placed my hand over her protruding belly and hummed softly, calming both mother and child."

I'd just heard the story behind the famous lullaby and why it soothed me; Hypatia was part of me.

"At that moment, I understood why Lucius's soul had not found a suitable host." Hypatia's voice amplified, commanding attention. "My blood gave him life; therefore, the host must also carry my blood. That night, so long ago, I constructed a dangerous plan. I played God, drawing out Lucius's soul and transferring it inside Brandon the day he was born; thereafter, altering lives and sealing Lucius's fate."

I knew the truth, heard it from my mom and from Eve, but the way Hypatia laid it out twisted the knife just a bit more. Now was my turn to demand an answer from her. "My mom remembers that day—the day I was born—the day you changed our lives. Why did you allow her to remember it? Why didn't you erase that memory too?"

Hypatia blinked, then an open stare came my way. "Because one day I would come for you, take you from your mother. What happened at your birth would remind her of this."

More sniffles came from Lindsey. I scooted closer, comforting her with an arm around her shoulders before I sassed back, "Me resisting wasn't part of your master plan, was it?"

She stared me down with eyes blazing. "No, it wasn't."

Kohath spoke up, taking charge of the conversation. "In our history, The Council has never witnessed a resurrection. This unprecedented event must be confirmed," Kohath challenged, before setting his sights on a female with long blonde hair hanging in her face, seated three chairs down from his.

"Athaliah, affirm Hypatia's words."

As she rose, her hair parted, revealing a pair of navy-colored orbs. She vanished from her seat, then reappeared in front of me so fast, I gasped and jerked backward. A smirk pulled at the corners of her mouth, then died as she demanded, "Hold out your hand."

No way was I gonna object; not with that frenzied go-postal gleam brightening her eyes. She speared my middle finger with her fang, drawing blood. I flinched at the sting, then did a double take as she squeezed a few drops into her mouth.

Her head snapped toward Hypatia. "Now you." Hypatia sighed, then flopped her hand in front of the crazed blonde. After performing the same ritual on Hypatia, she closed her eyes and stood very still. Seconds later, her eyelids flew open. "Hypatia speaks the truth; however, the blood revealed more. Lucius's soul lay dormant inside the host for many years, until an event in the boy's life triggered his awakening, an event of blood. Lucius's cravings have now become his host's cravings, the boy."

An image of Sam flashed in my mind, propelling me out of my seat. "An event? A nightmare is more like it. I didn't ask for this, and I sure as hell didn't agree to any of this. I want this thing out, now!"

Hypatia waved me away. "As I explained, you must become one with Lucius's soul. This will resolve your dilemma."

Rick darted in front of Hypatia like he was in a wheelchair race. "I hardly call that a solution. Life's not that black and white. There must be an alternative."

Lindsey sprang to her feet and shouted, "My brother is not going to become that thing you stuck inside him."

"That thing has a name, and it's Lucius," Hypatia fired back. "And Brandon *will* merge with him."

"Hypatia, even if their souls merge," the crazed blonde interjected, "it does not guarantee Lucius's survival."

Rick, Lindsey, Hypatia, Margarete, and Caleb sounded off at once. It became a bidding war of voices. Nothing made sense, just humming and buzzing rattling against my eardrums. I shouted over them. "One at a time!"

"Silence!" Kohath ordered. "Because one desires a certain outcome does not make it so. The Council must consider all options."

Margarete whispered into Caleb's ear, then jabbed an elbow into his side, nudging him forward.

He gave her a sneer before facing The Council. "May I offer a suggestion?"

Kohath nodded. "Of course, my son; however, I do believe the suggestion is Margarete's." His olive-colored eyes grew a shade brighter as they settled on her. "My dear, the binding ritual brought you into our family, and your abilities to subdue Caleb's recklessness has made me quite fond of you. Please, speak freely."

Did I even want to know what a binding ritual was? And was this guy really Caleb's dad? Whatever. Just skip to the part where we rid my body of the power, please.

Laughter snorted out of Caleb's mouth. "Reckless? There's not a reckless bone in my body."

Margarete exchanged a knowing look with Kohath before she kissed Caleb on the cheek. "Aw, you truly believe this."

She dissed Caleb before he could mutter a reply and bowed her head in Kohath's direction. "I am honored you think of me this way."

He acknowledged her with a slight smile. "Your suggestion?"

Margarete held her chin high as she addressed The Council. "Osiris and Isis reside within these very walls. Vampires of their stature may offer a solution we are unaware of. May we call on them to join us?"

An exaggerated head bob came from the crazed blonde. "Yes, of course. Kohath, we must send for them at once. They could be most helpful in this matter."

Kohath didn't say a word, just closed his eyes as if he were breaking into a bout of spiritual mediation. A quick second later, he announced, "They are on their way."

I glanced at Lindsey and Rick, offering them a shrug, then a whoosh of air sounded from across the room. My gaze darted in its direction and landed on a male and female, arm in arm, gliding through the door to the center of the room, their eyes glittering like jewels in the sunlight. My mom's favorite show popped into my head—the spinning door, the creepy music, and the voiceover, saying, "You've just crossed over into the *Twilight Zone*." I ditched the memory, then set my sights on the Johnny-come-latelies and heaved a sigh. I just didn't get how the Jim Morrison and Cleopatra doppelgangers were going to help my situation.

"Osiris, Isis, welcome," Kohath began. "The Council has been presented an extraordinary set of circumstances."

I gave them the once-over, him with his shaggy brown mane and her with her glitzy bangles and rings. My labels suited them. Besides, what the hell kind of names were Osiris and Isis? I was sticking with Jim Morrison and Cleopatra.

Caleb flapped a hand toward Hypatia, stealing Kohath's thunder. "Blue eyes here shoved her dead lover's soul into," he jutted a finger at me and plastered a "wait for it" look on his face, "Brandon. And Brandon wants the sucker out. Yep, that's about the gist of this little gathering."

Kohath dragged a hand over his face, then shook his head. Obviously, Caleb's commentary hadn't amused him.

Margarete rolled her eyes with exaggeration and silenced Caleb by pushing him down into a chair. "Unfortunately," she added, "he is correct, and this is our dilemma for which we will need your guidance."

Again, a whimper came from Lindsey, then another and another before she blurted out, "My brother has rights! He didn't choose this. This was forced on him."

I squeezed her hand. "It's okay, Lins." Out of the corner of my eye, Rick's pensive wrinkle cutting through his forehead made me wonder if he was having a *Twilight Zone* moment too?

The crazed blonde clapped her hands, demanding attention. "There is more. Hypatia's blood ties the boy and Lucius together, and this blood bond has strengthened over time. It will be most difficult to separate Lucius's soul from the boy." Jim Morrison chuckled, then exchanged looks with his counterpart, Cleopatra, before setting his sights on the crazed blonde. "There's always a loophole, dear Athaliah."

Her head tilted slightly as she studied him with her stone-cold, navy-colored orbs. "And what would this loophole be, Osiris?"

"Lucius's soul requires a host linked to Hypatia's blood, am I correct in my assumption?"

"You are," Hypatia butted in.

He left the crazed blonde's side and made his way over to Hypatia, resting his hand on her shoulder. "The loophole would be to create a new host and..." he glanced back at Cleopatra, a grin spreading across his lips. "...my beautiful wife can transfer Lucius's soul from the old host to the new one."

The bejeweled Cleopatra appeared at his side. "Brilliant idea, my love."

I cleared the lump building in my throat. "Um...you mean, take it out of me and put it in someone else?"

He thrust a hand in the air. "Exactly."

Kohath left his seat of power and walked the length of the table with his hands behind his back. After his third lap, he faced the doppelgangers. "Osiris, Isis, is there no other way?"

Cleopatra's tone was matter-of-fact. "A human host must merge with Lucius, either the current host or a new host. Those are the options." She raised her hand. "However, this does not guarantee Lucius's survival. A battle of the souls will occur. Whichever is the strongest will triumph over the other."

Hypatia gasped. "Wait. What?" Her voice tampered off as her eyes settled on me.

"I stated this earlier," the crazed blonde pointed out.

Hypatia quickly regained her composure. "Lucius will prevail. I'm certain of it."

"Well, I'm not going to be his stupid host or whatever you call it." I threw at her for the hundredth time.

"Yeah," Lindsey echoed.

Kohath rubbed at his temples. "Let me think."

One of Kohath's time warp companions rose from the table. I couldn't tell if his hair was black or blue, but he definitely had the same gleaming eyes as the rest of them. "Kohath, The Council must adjourn and discuss this matter privately."

"We will if necessary, Cain."

"Clearly, you need our help, Kohath, but we will patiently wait for your decision." Cleopatra glided along the floor on a course for the three of us. Her eyes twinkled as they traveled from me to Lindsey and to Rick. "And who might this trio be?"

I jabbed a finger in my chest. "I'm Brandon." I gave a head bob to my left. "This is my sister, Lindsey, and my friend, Rick."

We got a royal nod, then her gray orbs centered on me. "You must have parents—are they aware of your extracurricular activities? Maybe we should invite them to this little inquiry?"

Lindsey, Rick, and I shouted "No!" at the same time. I elaborated. "Our parents are not believers. My mom should, but she doesn't, so bringing them here would only freak them out." I threw a scowl at Lindsey. "I didn't even want her to come, but ya know, sisters. She threatened to tell."

Lindsey gave my shoulder a good nudge. "And I'd do it all over again too."

Rick cleared his throat, maybe in an attempt to have the floor. "I got kicked out of their house for suggesting Brandon had a vampire inside him, so unless you want more chaos erupting, I wouldn't include them."

A wide grin spread on her plum-colored lips. "We can't have that now, can we?" She didn't wait for a reply and spun around to face Kohath and his team. "Having a private discussion amongst yourselves will not alter the solution. A human host must be chosen, and it appears that young Brandon is not willing."

Hypatia blew out an impatient snort. "And where do you suppose we find a new host?"

I was with Hypatia on this one. "It's not like they're lining up at the door."

"I say we hit the bars and round up a few drunk humans," Caleb chimed in. "Hypatia can have her pick."

"Be serious," Margarete scolded.

He offered up his palms with a shrug. "I was." She shushed him with a finger to his lips.

"Finding a human open to becoming a host will not be an easy task," Kohath said, agreeing with me and Hypatia.

"Like I said," Caleb began but fell mute by a swift glare from Margarete.

"I'm screwed," I mumbled, sinking into my chair.

"I'll do it," Rick blurted out in a determined tone, like he'd already thought it all through.

Caleb slapped a hand against his thigh. "Ha!"

Silence swept over the room, with all eyes on Rick; especially Hypatia's. Her ocean-blue orbs lit up like the Fourth of July.

I closed my gaping mouth, did a double take, then hit the rewind button in my brain. Yep, he definitely said it, but I couldn't let him. I bolted to his side, where I shook my head so hard it hurt. "I can't let you do this, Rick."

Hypatia appeared next to him in under a second. He glanced at her, then focused on me as he gripped my hand. "I'm not doing it for you, Brandon." He touched his smooth face once marred with scars. "I'm doing this for me. What if I could walk again, get out of this chair? Man, that's like a second chance."

Hypatia gazed down at him, spreading her lips into a slow smile. "I'm pleased with this new host. I accept."

"It's not your decision!" I screamed at her, spewing spit. "Your blood healed his face! He's not thinking straight!"

Lindsey neared me and rested her hand on my shoulder. "Maybe he is."

Rick squeezed my hand, forcing me to look at him. "Brandon," he said in a calm, steady voice. "You're right, I'm in awe of what Hypatia's blood can do, but I'm quite aware of what I'm committing to."

"Are you?" Kohath asked, joining the conversation. "I think not."

Hypatia whirled around and bared her fangs. "Must you always interfere in my life, Kohath!"

The muscles in his jaw clenched as he locked eyes with her. "Hypatia, as much as you'd like to think so, the world does not revolve around you." He sighed. "In order to make a rational decision, this young man must be informed of our rules and our complex world."

"Excuse me," Rick called out, pushing his wheelchair between them. "I know a lot more than you think. I'm a teacher, research is my thing. In Brandon's case, my research led me into a whole other world, a world of darkness, blood, killing, sacrifice, and pain. I might not know your rules, but believe me, I've got a good handle on your world."

Hypatia leveled her gaze on him and flashed the flirtiest smile I'd ever seen. "You intrigue me, Scholar Rick."

A deep rose color creeped across Rick's cheeks as he said, "Thank you. I'll take that as a compliment."

Was he into her? I gave him a good squint—flushed face, silly grin, swallowing a thousand times. Yep, affirmative. He was totally into her.

Kohath's voice bellowed into the room, pulling the plug on my examination of Rick. "The Council will vote, and the outcome will determine if Rick is a suitable host."

A dark storm brewed inside Hypatia's ocean-blue eyes as she spat out one name. "Kohath!"

I totally got why she was pissed off. Could they even do that? Just as I was contemplating the thought, Rick zipped over to the table and sounded off. "Have any of you people heard of free will? When it comes to my life, *I* make my own choices, not this table of dictators."

Hypatia whipped her head in Rick's direction, that smug demeanor morphing into a look of sheer adoration, as if she could never look away. She placed herself at his side, held her chin high, and defied her brother's order. "My decision and Rick's are firm. We will not comply with your demands, Kohath."

Kohath's thick pale brows lifted to his hairline. "These are not my demands, but those of The Council."

Jim Morrison strolled up and laid a hand on his shoulder. "Kohath, this is no longer a matter for The Council, and Hypatia is fortunate to have a willing host."

His counterpart, Cleopatra, quickly seconded his words. "Indeed, she is." She too rested a hand on Kohath's shoulder. "Hypatia seems to have a connection with the young man, and he to her. This is a good thing, Kohath."

The guy with the blue-black hair approached Kohath, pressing his fingertips together as he spoke. "Kohath, we sympathize with you. Hypatia is of your blood, mortal and immortal. However, we agree. The Council's mediation is no longer required."

Kohath's gaze drifted and settled on Hypatia. "My emotions got the better of me." A slight nod dipped his chin as he faced the doppelgangers. "Osiris, Isis, a new host has been chosen. You may proceed."

Hypatia and Rick locked eyes, smiles spreading across their lips. I did a double take. What just happened? Was I free? But at what cost? "No," I cried, then pushed Hypatia away from Rick.

She stumbled a step or two before righting herself. Margarete and Caleb dashed in my direction, but the doppelgangers beat them, each latching onto my arms and dragging me back into my chair.

"Let him go!" Lindsey shrieked, charging to my side, throwing a protective arm around me.

"Everyone, calm down!" Kohath barked out the order like a drill sergeant.

"It's okay, let him go!" Rick shouted over the commotion, wheeling his chair next to mine. "Brandon, it's okay. I'm okay." He waited for me to look him in the eyes. "I want this, I do."

I searched his face for truth in his words. "But you're giving up your life...and the power! What if it takes over your soul?" I shook my head hard. "No, I can't let you do this."

"Brandon, I'm aware of the risks and I accept them. I've been through a lot in my life. It's made me a tough son of a bitch. I'm prepared to fight for my soul."

My chin trembled as I choked down a slew of sobs. "B-but, what if you lose?"

Lindsey started blubbering and hid her face in her hands.

"That could happen," Rick said matter-of-factly, "but I got this feeling I'll be okay." His hands rested on his knees. "And if it means I can walk again..."

I nodded and grimaced at the same time. He seemed sure, and I got that he wanted to walk again, but if the power took over, he'd never know.

Caleb spoke up and painted a clear picture for me. "Look, you've got two choices: turn yourself or let Rick turn. Those are your options."

Lindsey gave my arm a squeeze. "I want my brother back. Rick wants this, so give it to him, please!"

Seeing my little sister's unsmiling face tugged at my heart. I wanted myself back too. So much so, I finally gave in. "Okay."

Lindsey flung her arms around me and hugged me tight.

Rick gripped my shoulder and gave it a good squeeze.

Hypatia let out a gasp, then avowed, "I will take care of Rick, I promise."

"Isis," Kohath called the bejeweled Cleopatra to his side. "What is needed for the transfer of souls?"

She gave a tilt of her head, and her jet-black hair fell to one side. "Very little; a drop of blood, a pinch of flesh, a strand of hair, a rope, a circle of salt, and my oils. However, considering the nature of the spell, I must channel my magic for its complexity." Her gray orbs took stock of the three of us. "You should feed them, let them rest. In the morning, I shall begin the transfer."

"Thomas," Kohath addressed a vampire standing in the background. "Escort our guests to the slumbering chambers and have the staff prepare their meal of choice."

"Yes, Kohath," he answered as he approached us, clad in a floor-length robe like the rest of the time warp clan.

Rick cocked his head. "Wait a minute...meal of choice? You stock groceries? Human groceries?"

Kohath chuckled. "A well-stocked kitchen to be exact, with a full staff."

Rick's brows gathered deeper.

"What kind of hosts would we be if we sent our human blood donors on their way without rejuvenating their strength?" Kohath admonished.

"So, you feed them; hence the stocked kitchen and our meal of choice," Rick surmised.

"You are correct, Rick," Kohath concurred. "Now please, go with Thomas."

Thomas fixed his deep-set eyes on the three of us, and his bushy blond hair bounced as he nodded toward the door. "Come."

As I followed behind Thomas, an image of a monk flashed in my head. Apparently, thou shalt not wear Levi's or T-shirts was a thing here. He led us to a hallway lit by lanterns, then slipped inside the dim passageway followed by Rick, then Lindsey. I brought up the rear. Thomas trekked along, like he'd traveled the walkway a thousand times, guiding us through every twist and turn until we arrived at a spiral staircase. "This way, please," he said, directing us up the stairs.

At the top, yet another hallway came into view, this one littered with closed doors on either side. Thomas stopped midway, then selected a door to his left and shooed us inside. A wood-carved sofa and two chairs dressed up the front room. "Here you have a small sitting area." In two steps, he stood inside the pale gray kitchen. "Full kitchen." He spun around, zipping down a small hall before pushing open one of two doors. "The bedroom." His eyes landed on us. "With three twin beds, one for each of you." He opened the opposite door. "The bathroom." He gestured toward the ivory vanity. "On the bottom shelves are additional towels."

My stomach released a low growl. I sucked it in, trying to shut it up. "Sorry."

He squished his eyebrows together and stared at me like the sound of hunger was foreign to him. After a brief pause, he returned to his chatter. "Have you any luggage?"

"No," Rick answered. "It was a sudden trip."

"Very well. The staff is ready to prepare your meal. What should I tell them you would like?"

"Burger and fries," Lindsey blurted out first. "Oh, and well-done, please. Also, can I have a Coke?" "Of course," Thomas said with a nod.

"That sounds super good, Lins." I turned to Thomas. "I'll have the same."

"Make that three," Rick chimed in.

Thomas's eyes altered into a blinding hue, then it was gone. "I have conveyed your orders. The staff will bring your food shortly. Is there anything else you need before I leave?"

"I'm good, thanks," I said.

"Me too," Lindsey mimicked.

"Thank you, we're good," Rick affirmed.

His lips spread into something that resembled a smile, then he bowed and left us alone.

Lindsey went straight into the kitchen and started pulling open drawers until she found plates, silverware, and napkins. As she set the island for dinner, she said, "It's like our own mini apartment."

"Time warp style, with ancient wood furniture and frilly drapes," I added.

Rick smirked, then bobbed his head in agreement. "They do seem to be stuck in a different era."

"I think they're beautiful," Lindsey said, pulling out the barstools, "like antiques."

"You got that right," I mumbled.

A soft knock at the door grabbed our attention. Rick plastered a deep frown on his face. "No way they could've made the food that fast."

"Well, they do everything else super-fast," I said as I pulled the door open.

Hypatia stood in the doorway with her hands fluttering at her sides, and her ocean-blue eyes wide. "May I speak to Rick?"

I glanced over my shoulder and set my gaze on him. He gave me a thumbs-up. I turned back to her. "Come in."

She shook her head with a defiant no. "I cannot."

Rick was already at the door, nudging me aside. "What is it, Hypatia?"

She backed up and waved him into the hallway. "In private, please."

He left the room, stopping inches from her. At once, she knelt in front of him, covering his hands with hers. She spoke softly, her words intended for Rick and Rick alone. He gripped her hands and murmured something in her ear. Her body shuddered, then she kissed his cheek and rose to her feet. He sat still, watching her walk away. Only when she was out of sight did he come back inside.

"What was that about?" I probed.

He waved me away. "It was nothing."

"It didn't look like nothing to me," Lindsey smirked and anchored a hand on her hip.

"Do you two know the meaning of the word private?"

I huffed, then pointed out, "You don't even know each other. What's there to be private about?"

"I'm not going to betray her trust, but what I will say is this, I'm a little less nervous than I was."

Lindsey flapped a hand in the air. "Oh, yeah, like that really tells us something."

Rick shrugged. "Sorry, that's all you guys get."

Lindsey blew him off and went back into the kitchen.

Wheels clinking against the wood floor and a whiff of grilled burgers and fresh cut fries turned my head toward the open door. Two women, with aprons draped over their clothes, stood just outside the doorway, a cart on wheels between them. No old-fashioned gowns or unnatural eyes there, just pure human beings. "Dinner is ready," the taller of the two said. "May we come in?"

"Yeah, sure, come in." I gestured toward the kitchen.

They began removing lids from dishes, then set a tray of grilled burgers and a basket of crisp fries in the center of the island. Three liters of Coke and a bucket of ice came next, along with every kind of condiment I could think of. Hunger stirred in my stomach once again, and I licked my lips.

"You're all set. Enjoy," the shorter one offered.

"Thank you," Rick said.

"Welcome." They left us to our meal and closed the door behind them.

Like a pack of wolves, we surrounded the island, piling food onto our plates. Lindsey took a huge bite and moaned.

"Oh my God, this is sooo good!"

"Yeah," I mumbled with a mouthful of food.

"I didn't realize I was this hungry," Rick agreed, inhaling a few fries.

I glanced at Rick and a frown cut through my forehead.

"This is gonna sound morbid, but..."

Rick's eyes locked on mine. "But what?"

"Dude, this is like our last supper."

Lindsey choked on her food, then gasped out, "Brandon!" Rick pressed his lips together in a slight grimace, then gave a soft nod. "Well, technically, it is my last meal."

I swallowed hard and pushed my plate away. "It could be mine too. What if something goes wrong? What if we don't make it?"

Lindsey's eyes bulged as she popped off the barstool. "Don't say that! Don't even think that!" Her bottom lip quivered. "I miss Mom and Dad," she cried, then ran into the bathroom.

I bolted after her, and got the door slammed in my face. "Lins, I'm sorry. Please, open the door."

"Go away!"

"She has a right to be scared, Brandon," Rick insisted.

I threw him my most annoyed glare and faced the door again. "I'm an idiot, okay. If you won't come out, at least let me bring you your dinner. You need to eat."

The door flew open, and she purposely stood in front of me, sneering. Not until I lowered my gaze did she release me from her wrath and march over to the barstool. She took a swig of Coke, then bit into her burger, keeping her eyes on her plate.

I shoved my hands into my pockets and stepped toward her. Rick pursed his lips. He was probably right; I should let her be. I reclaimed my seat and shoved my burger in my mouth.

Afterward, I helped Lindsey clear the island and load the small dishwasher. She continued to give me the silent treatment, and I didn't press it. She knew I was sorry, and I'd prepared her for something going wrong if it did.

CHAPTER 14

Early in the morning, distant knocking forced its way into my dream. I stood alone, facing a black door.

The tapping grew louder, but I still did nothing to answer it. It became insistent, pounding hard and fast. My eyelashes fluttered open as I sat straight up, my gaze darting about the room. The knocking persisted. I shook off the haze of sleep. It wasn't a dream. "Hang on," I shouted, jumping off the bed and stumbling toward the door. I pulled it open to find Thomas standing there, a serious expression plastered on his face.

"Isis is ready," he said, motioning toward the hallway.

"Um...can you give us a few minutes? I need to wake Rick and Lindsey."

He bowed his head. "Of course."

I waved him inside. "I'll go tell them." I left him in the front room, then hurried into the bedroom. I shook Rick but kept a good grip on his shoulder so he wouldn't fall off the bed.

"What is it? What's wrong?" he rattled off as he grabbed onto my arm and sat up. His eyes found mine. "It's time, isn't it?"

"Yes," I said, then helped him into the wheelchair. Next, I went to Lindsey. As I gently shook her, I called out her name.

"Lindsey."

Her hand flapped me away.

"Lins, c'mon, we gotta go."

Her eyelids flew open. "What? Yeah, yeah, okay." She scurried out of bed, brushing off her clothes.

"Thomas is waiting for us."

Lindsey plastered her hands to her cheeks. "Oh, God."

I wrapped my arm around her shoulders and hugged her. "I'm scared too."

"Group hug," Rick said, spreading his arms. Lindsey and I flung our arms around him. Lindsey started blubbering, and I joined in. Rick was the strong one. "Everything will be okay, you'll see."

I sucked in a breath, wanting to share his optimism because everything *had* to be okay, and...today was my birthday.

A knock came on the bedroom door. "Please, we must get going," Thomas urged through its frame.

I gave Rick one last hug, swiped away my tears, then headed for the door. Lindsey stuck to my side, her hand gripping my arm. Rick hesitated for a brief second, then gave the wheels of the chair a good spin. The three of us faced Thomas, like a trio of superheroes ready to save the world.

"Come," Thomas said, ushering us into the hallway.

Once again, we trudged after Thomas as he led us back through the lantern-lit hallway, all the way to the solid black door trimmed in silver. A soft whoosh escaped the door as Thomas pushed it open.

As we entered, a strained hush fell over the crowded room. The time warp clan sat behind their marble table, with Kohath dead center. More throne-like chairs, placed near the clan, held Caleb, Margarete, and Hypatia. Hypatia's pale expression and flighty hands didn't give me much hope. Not so with Jim Morrison and his sidekick, Cleopatra; they stood tall, shoulders back, chests out, expelling confidence. A small table cluttered with odd items peeked out from behind them, and off to their right lay a large ring of something that looked like salt on the polished floor.

"What the hell are they gonna do with that?" I whispered to Rick.

His gaze darted back and forth between Hypatia and the salt-like stuff. "I have no idea."

Lindsey's brow twitched, and a shudder ran through her as she spotted the ring on the floor. "This can't be happening, especially on your birthday."

I pried her hand off my arm so I could wrap it around her. "It's okay, Lins."

"Isis." Kohath's voice boomed inside the room, drawing my attention from Lindsey to him. "You may begin the transformation."

My heart jumped into my throat. I wasn't about to go into this thing blind. "Wait! What's gonna happen? I need like a preview or something."

"I'd like to know too," Rick echoed.

Kohath nodded. "Isis, I believe this is a reasonable request. If you will, please inform them."

Her eyes brightened as she strutted over to us. "I will speak plainly. Do forgive me if I frighten you." Too late. I was officially creeped out.

"Blood, salt, oils, rope, and my magic will force Lucius's soul from Brandon and into Rick."

Force? That hardly seemed necessary. The power had stayed pretty quiet since we'd gotten here. I felt I had to enlighten her. "I haven't felt the power...um, I mean, Lucius at all. Maybe this is the moment he's been waiting for."

Her eyes narrowed as she waved my theory away. "*Or it's a warning; the calm before the storm. We must assume nothing.*"

I heaved a sigh. *Thank you, Miss Optimistic.*

Her probing gaze lingered on me until I squirmed. She smirked, then centered her attention on Rick and Hypatia. "Hypatia, after Lucius's soul enters Rick, you must turn him at once." She paused and gathered her perfect eyebrows together. "This will initiate the battle of the souls."

Hypatia grabbed at her throat and shivered. "Battle?"

Rick shifted in the wheelchair, and I could've sworn he flinched. "A literal battle?" he clarified. "And for how long?"

Cleopatra shrugged, as if it meant nothing. "I cannot say. We are in unfamiliar territory. As you humans say, we are winging it."

A large wrinkle cut through Rick's forehead as he jerked his head toward her. "Winging it?"

I called the dynamic duo out. "You said you could do this."

Jim Morrison gave a firm nod. "And we can."

Everyone started talking at once, and a buzz of words circled the room. Kohath pushed to his feet, clapping his hands. "Silence!" He whipped his head toward Hypatia and plastered one hefty scowl on his face. "This is your doing." She seemed peeved, folding her arms in a huff and throwing a hostile look his way. He turned his back on her and quickly faced me and Rick. "Isis's power reaches far beyond the human grasp. I have every confidence in her abilities."

"Today's Brandon's birthday!" Lindsey blurted out. "You'd better have confidence in her."

Kohath lifted his thick brows, then shifted his olive-colored orbs on me, before centering them again on Lindsey. "I assure you, I do."

Cleopatra acknowledged Lindsey with a downturned smile, and not in a sarcastic way, but more sympathetic. She appeared at my side, taking my face into her cold hands. "And a memorable birthday it will be, the day I free you of Lucius's soul."

"And ensure our safety," I insisted.

She shrugged halfheartedly, taking a long pause before rattling off, "Yes, of course." Her jeweled fingers pointed toward the ring of salt. "Shall we begin?"

I inhaled a deep breath before answering. "Okay."

Rick wheeled closer to me and gave an unwavering, "Yes."

A smug grin formed on her lips as she said, "Come into the circle where you will lay side by side." She gave a quick jerk of her jet-black hair toward her comrade. "Osiris, please help Rick into the circle."

Lindsey gasped out loud and latched onto me. "Noooo!" Margarete appeared and wedged us apart. Her violet eyes leveled on Lindsey, growing blindingly bright as she spoke.

"Relax. Let everything go." Lindsey fell silent, her arms dropping to her sides as she flopped down into a chair. Margarete glanced my way. "She's fine."

Lindsey sat so unnaturally quietly, as if she were in a druglike haze. Not conscious of what was about to take place was better for Lindsey, and with her out of harm's way, I could focus all my attention on the task at hand, ridding my body of the power.

I entered the ring of salt, lifting my chin and acting all cool, while hiding the clammy sweat building between my clasped palms. My legs wobbled, and I stumbled to the floor with a thud, pulling the plug on my laid-back sham. Rick had already claimed his spot, thanks to the strong arms of Jim Morrison. As I stretched out next to Rick, I wanted to say something deep, but two lame words came out. "Thank you."

Rick gripped my hand, squeezing hard. "Don't thank me, Brandon. I want this."

Cleopatra loomed over us, her eyes adjusting like camera lenses. "It's my turn to speak and for you to listen." She snatched up a jar filled with oil off the small table. A silver dagger floating inside clanked against the glass. "With this blade, I will draw blood from each of you, including Hypatia." She gave a nod toward some coiled up rope on the table. "I will dip this rope in your blood and use it to bind Rick and Brandon until Lucius's soul has been transferred." Her gray orbs landed on Hypatia. "At that time, I will instruct Hypatia to turn Rick." She paused, her gaze traveling from Hypatia to Rick, then me. "This will set in motion the battle of souls, and then we wait. It could be days, weeks, or months before we have a victor."

She fished out the dagger and ordered, "Hypatia, come."

Hypatia strutted over with confidence. "My palm, Isis."

Cleopatra radiated authority as she buried the silver dagger into Hypatia's flesh. Hypatia held a strong stance, but the tears pooling in her eyes gave away her pain.

"Osiris, fetch the ceremonial bowl and hold it beneath Hypatia's hand."

"Of course, my dear." Before he even finished his words, he had placed a gold-leafed bowl below Hypatia's hand, catching the droplets of her blood.

Seconds passed before she shooed Hypatia away. "I have what I need."

Hypatia pressed her thumb against her wound and walked with grace to the safety of her chair. I caught an exchange of glances between Kohath and Hypatia and thought of Lindsey. I twisted my head around to get a glimpse of her. That faraway gaze still held her expression, and I found comfort in that.

"Rick, drink from the bowl. Swallow two mouthfuls. Hypatia's blood must swim inside you before I dagger your palm."

Hypatia whirled around and blocked my view of Lindsey. "Isis, this is not necessary," she challenged. "My blood entered Rick's veins when I smeared it on his face to heal his scars."

"Hypatia, a few drops are hardly enough to contain Lucius." Cleopatra paused to twist her plum-colored lips into a sneer. "But thank you, dear, for your advice."

Hypatia retaliated with a curtsy before returning to her seat.

Cleopatra ignored Hypatia's mockery and lifted the bowl to Rick's lips. "Drink until I tell you to stop."

As Rick chugged Hypatia's blood like beer, I leaned in and took a whiff—nothing. No mouthwatering hunger, feverish shivering, or spike in my pulse. My heart thumped along, content as ever; and the *only* one rattling my eardrums. What the hell? Was the power gone? Had it already moved on to Rick? I gave my head a firm shake. If only I could be so lucky.

"Stop!" Cleopatra's shrill voice barged into my brain, shoving my thoughts aside. I turned an eye on Rick just as she skewered his palm.

He belted out a weighty grunt, then mumbled, "Jesus."

Jim Morrison, her partner in crime, quickly tucked the bowl under the steady stream of Rick's blood, not missing a drop. As he glanced her way, his brown orbs shimmered with light. "You never cease to amaze me, my dear."

A beautiful smile stretched beyond her cheeks, then it was gone. "Save your flattery, Osiris, I've only just begun. Besides, the young man's palm needs the aid of your gifts." He speared his finger with a fang, smirked, then smeared the bloody tip across Rick's palm.

Rick's blood shrank backward as a blanket of new skin covered the wound. A huge breath escaped his lungs as he glanced at me. "I ain't gonna lie, man. It hurts like a son of a bitch."

Cleopatra took my hand. "Now you, Brandon."

As the dagger pinched the center of my palm, my insides twisted, and I grew ice cold. I couldn't focus or feel my body. My mind drifted, and suddenly I was outside myself, looking in.

My immortal soul ignited, spewing my cold-blooded strength inside the boy. Isis had been accurate with her perception of a warning. I'd been lying low waiting for an opportunity, and there it was. I manipulated the boy's hand with a flick of his wrist, snatching the knife away from Isis. One by one, I curled his fingers around the cold metal, then aimed it at Hypatia. With the boy's voice, I shouted, "How dare you offer a cripple to house my superior spirit!"

Hypatia's jaw hinged open, and the tiniest of sounds escaped her. She recovered quickly, blasting from her chair and sending it tumbling backward as she bolted toward me. Her pesky brother yanked her back with a strong arm.

"Still quite the meddling brother I see. Kohath, you old devil you." I twisted the boy's face into a wonderful sneer. "I'll simply come to her." I clasped the boy's hands loosely behind his back and broke into a stride. His shoes plowed into an invisible barrier, tossing the boy backward and me off a step or two.

Isis snickered, then spread her plum-colored lips into a victorious grin. "My ring of salt confines you, Lucius."

I bobbed the boy's head in acknowledgment and set his sights on the resourceful witch. "You're clever, Isis, yet..." I paused the boy's voice to add a touch of drama, before pointing the dagger's tip at his throat. "I'm cunning. One slice and I'll have my host."

What the hell? I have a knife to my neck, people! Why wasn't anyone stopping me? Couldn't they tell I wasn't me! I stood frozen, watching the horrible scene unfold with no control over my body, my voice, my words. I needed Lindsey to scream bloody murder, but vampire charm had her on the off switch.

The boy's eye caught a flicker of Osiris's shaggy mane. I whipped his body around and confronted him. "Every step equals an inch of blade, Osiris."

Warm fluid trickled down my neck. That had to be blood! I didn't feel pain. Why didn't I feel pain? An assault of adrenaline spurted inside me, jerking me forward. The world came rushing back; shoes skidding against the polished floor, a muddle of voices blasting out high-pitched shrieks, and my skin throbbing with a feverish burn beneath the blade jammed in my neck. Freedom! I have my freedom.

I didn't waste a single second of it and belted out, "Help me!" I'd barely gotten the words out when the power yanked the cord on my independence.

With the boy's free hand, I jutted toward the herd of vampires scurrying my way, and the other kept the dagger securely embedded into his neck. "Stay back!" The cripple laying inches from the boy's feet peered up at him, with nostrils flaring and breaths rasping. He hardly presented a threat. Osiris, Isis, and Athaliah were my worthy opponents. I kept the boy's gaze on that trio.

"Lucius," Isis began, in her holier-than-thou tone. "The host has been chosen, a willing host anointed with Hypatia's blood."

"These menacing gestures are without foundation. The moment Isis summons the dagger, it will return to her," Osiris conveyed with a predictable smirk.

"Thank you for that insight, Osiris. However, the blade is still in the boy's possession which leads me to believe Isis is aware of the risk in recalling it." As Osiris wiped the pompous expression off his face, I bent the boy's body into a bow, mocking the Ruler of the Dead and the Mistress of Magic.

"Your objection to this host is moot," Athaliah argued, leveling her navy-colored eyes on the boy's. "As a human, he is confined to a wheelchair. As a vampire, his legs will take powerful strides."

I raised the boy's shoulders and projected his voice. "For centuries, my soul searched for a permanent host. Most have not been able to survive it until this boy."

"Hypatia's blood is the key, not the host," Athaliah persisted. "Do you want to live in the body of a 17-year-old boy or the body of a man?"

"The boy suits me." I cast the boy's eyes on the cripple. "He does not."

Hypatia flung her arms wildly and broke free from Kohath's clutches. She charged forward, clenching and unclenching her fists. At the ring's edge, she turned her ocean-blue orbs into dark slits. "Lucius, I have lived through those centuries with you, fighting at your side to breathe life back into your soul, yet if you choose to slice Brandon's throat, I will let him bleed out and watch your banished soul drift into the atmosphere. So, choose wisely, my love."

As I gazed at her through the boy's eyes, tracing the resolve etched into her beautiful face, I had no doubt she meant every word. In a single breath, I surrendered the dagger to Isis, laid the boy's body next to the cripple and let the boy resurface.

The thump of my heart grew softer, turning down the volume of tension. Sensations came flooding back, summoning the throbbing sting to resurface full force in the side of my neck. I belted out a groan and grabbed the base of my throat. My fingers slipped on something warm and wet...*my blood*!

Cleopatra leaned over me, then jabbed a fang into her finger, squeezing out blood and pressing the moist tip against my neck. "My blood is a rare gift, young mortal, yet necessary to heal such a wound."

The gripping pinches of biting pain vanished. I pushed out one more moan, then inhaled several breaths of relief. "Thank you." I quickly stuck out my hand to her. "Let's finish this."

"Agreed." Her gray orbs brightened as she thrust the dagger into my palm, spilling my blood into the bowl.

A volcano of heat set my palm on fire. I clenched every muscle, fighting to shake off the smarting burn. The pain from the dagger was nothing if it got my life back. Besides, Rick wanted the power and he could have it. *Good riddance.*

"I bind you with blood." Cleopatra's voice swelled inside my ears, drowning out all sound and demanding attention. "I bind you with flesh," she chanted, coiling a blood-soaked rope around my wrist and Rick's. She immersed her hands into the bloody bowl, then let them drip over Rick and me. "With this blood, I fuse these souls; three become two, two become one. I bind you with blood. I bind you with flesh." She gripped our bound wrists, raising them over her head. "With this blood, I fuse these souls; three become two, two become one. Rise, Lucius." She cranked up the voice dial, spouting off gibberish as her eyes rolled back in her head.

My foot twitched, then my hand. Spasms jerked my body off the floor, then every inch of me shook, hard. I couldn't stop it. I grabbed Rick's arm with my free hand. "What's happening?"

Rick lay motionless, his mouth hanging open, a glob of drool hanging off his lip.

Something tugged at my gut. There it was again and again. My stomach cramped, bulged, and erupted, like something was trying to get out. The pressure inched upward, crushing my lungs. I thrashed about on the cold floor, gasping for air, with one hand bound to Rick's and the other gripping his arm. The force kept climbing, reaching my throat and spilling into my mouth, forcing it wide open. I let loose a gut-wrenching scream, and a flood of gray haze slithered out with it. The thick fog hovered over me, twisting and turning, searching for something or someone.

Cleopatra stepped into its path, looping the snake-like vapor around her bloody hands, chanting, "Renewal, rebirth, reform."

As she rattled on, sweat oozed from my pores, throwing a feverish ache across my body. A persistent heaviness trapped my arms and legs, and I barely managed to turn my head toward Rick.

Cleopatra opened her hands, then unraveled the gray haze into Rick's gaping mouth. As the last of it vanished, she ordered, "Now, Hypatia!"

Hypatia fell to her knees next to Rick, hesitated for a brief second, then sank her pearly fangs into his flesh. The wet sloshing of his blood filling her mouth jammed the circuits in my brain. A gallon of sweat unleashed on my body, pooling around me. Spots altered my vision, then cleared, allowing me a glimpse of Hypatia squeezing her own blood into Rick's mouth. *I'm gonna get sick.* My eyelids slid closed.

CHAPTER 15

When I opened my eyes, Lindsey's tearstained face came into view. She locked her arms around my neck, squeezing me harder than ever. Words left her lips as strangled sobs, then cleared. "I saw everything! I couldn't move, couldn't talk, but I knew...I'm sorry. I'm sorry."

I hugged her back, my own voice threatening to crack. "I'm..." I forced the waterworks back down. "I'm okay, Lins, and it's me who should be sorry. I should have never let you come." My gaze wandered over her shoulder and across the room, landing on Jim Morrison, Cleopatra, Margarete, and Caleb. I bolted upright, knocking Lindsey off-balance. With one hand I steadied her, while the other one flailed toward the righteous duo. "Where's Rick? What happened to Rick?"

Jim Morrison stepped forward and offered up, "He's resting. Hypatia and Kohath are with him."

My gaze went back and forth between the vampires. Caleb seemed to be the brutally honest one of the bunch, so I directed my next question to him. "Is Rick still...Rick?"

A halfhearted shrug lifted Caleb's shoulders before he replied. "Lucius appears to have the upper hand."

A feeble "No," slipped out of my mouth as my stomach twisted into a huge knot.

Cleopatra flapped her fingers in Caleb's direction. "The battle has just begun. Neither Lucius nor Rick has the upper hand." She turned to me. "Your question may not be answered for days, weeks, or even months."

I weighed her words in my mind. Had she just said them to appease me? "Is that true? What you said?"

She arched her perfect eyebrows at me. "Deceiving you serves no purpose. Of course, it's true."

I narrowed my gaze, studying her. I'd never get past that poker-faced expression of hers. The only way I'd know for sure was to see Rick myself. "Take me to Rick. I want to see him."

Caleb dismissed my idea with a slow head shake. "He's transitioning and locked and loaded with an ancient vampire soul."

Jim Morrison and Cleopatra bobbed their heads in agreement, but I wasn't taking no for an answer. "I'm not asking. Either take me to him or I'll find him myself."

Caleb chuckled, then slapped me on the back. "You got some balls on you, kid."

Margarete nudged Caleb aside while shaking her head. "Brandon might have a point," she offered, seeming to come to my defense. "Isis, seeing Brandon may call forth Rick."

Cleopatra's eyes brightened as she acknowledged the vampire. "Excellent point, Margarete."

Margarete spread her lips into a smug grin as she jammed an elbow into Caleb's side.

Whatever rivalry was going on between them, I could care less. I pushed them aside and demanded, "Take me to him."

Lindsey let out a mousy shriek. "I can't do it. I can't see anymore. I can't, I can't, I can't."

I hooked my arm around her shoulders, pausing her trembling. "You don't have to. Wait here."

Margarete appeared and brushed a strand of hair off Lindsey's forehead, then tucked her under her arm. "Caleb and I will stay with her." Margarete shooed me away. "Go. Osiris and Isis will take you."

I hugged Lindsey and assured, "I'll be back as soon as I can."

"Okay," she whispered.

As I walked out the door, I glanced back at Lindsey. She plastered a meek smile on her face and waved a shaky hand. This was my fault, even though I'd begged her not to come. But she'd gotten her way, as always, and she hadn't given me much choice. After all this was over and we were back home, I'd make it up to her somehow. I waved back, then headed after the duo.

"A stairwell at the end of this hall leads to the immortal chambers," Cleopatra announced before resting her hands on my shoulders, detaining me with a leveled gaze. "The outcome you seek may not be the outcome you receive. You must prepare yourself for that."

I held up a firm hand. "I got it. Just take me to him."

"As you wish."

As I kept up with their quick strides, her words of warning occupied my brain, growing louder and louder until I could no longer ignore them. She was right, I couldn't just walk in there and demand Rick's presence. I knew Lucius's strength firsthand. If he was the one I laid eyes on, then I'd have to be smart and back off. Because what if he tried to take my life again? The saliva inside my mouth evaporated as that thought intensified. I glanced at my escorts. "Um...what happens if—"

"It's only Lucius?" she said, finishing my sentence.

I cleared my dry throat. "Yes."

"Rick's body is too weak to move. Lucius must wait out the transformation period, but we will protect you should he threaten you." She furrowed her brows. "Do you still wish to go forward?"

I didn't hesitate. "Yeah, I gotta do this. I need to see him. I need to know."

"Very well."

****

Inside the dim stairwell, the soles of our shoes brushed against the metal rungs as we spiraled downward. I trudged a step or two behind the duo, running scenarios through my head. Did I ask questions or let him speak? Say nothing, get close enough to look into his eyes? Regardless of what Cleopatra had said, I knew I couldn't underestimate him, and I wasn't about to become a vampire snack. The one scenario that stuck with me—don't get too close but close enough to catch a glimmer of Rick.

We'd rounded the stairwell a dozen times before the second-floor landing made its appearance. Jim Morrison veered toward the door. The hinges groaned as he yanked it open, releasing an icy gust of air from the second floor. He crossed the threshold of the undead first, then Cleopatra, then me. The hallway mirrored the one I'd just come from, nothing special. Then again, vampires rested on the other side of those doors, so yeah, totally incomparable. As Jim Morrison's hand surrounded one of the gold latches, my heartbeat hit the pause button, then slammed against my chest.

Cleopatra and Jim Morrison stood on either side of me and ushered me inside the room. Kohath's thick brows twisted into a scowl. "Osiris, Isis, what is the meaning of this?"

Jim Morrison approached Kohath with a slow, steady gait. "Relax, he—"

"I insisted," I interrupted. "This was my idea." I pushed through them, my gaze ping-ponging over the obsolete furnishings, before landing on Rick sprawled out on an enormous four-poster bed, shooting his mouth off.

"The power of vampire blood is rushing through my veins. I hear everything, see everything, sense everything. I'm once again one with the world. I am complete." His voice had mutated, sounding smug, cold, and arrogant. The carefree, causal Rick I knew was gone, but still, I had to make certain and inched closer to the bed, narrowing my eyes. Not one scar marred his new, flawless complexion, and the bald spots once scattered across his scalp were replaced with thick, shiny hair.

Hypatia sat by his side in some old-fashioned gaudy chair, heaving sighs and rolling those ocean-blue eyes of hers.

After waiting centuries to reunite with her long-lost love, she seemed less than pleased. Had her hopes been too high?

Had the time apart changed him or her? Was the person lying in that bed not who she expected? The secret conversation between Rick and Hypatia resurfaced inside my brain. Had she told Rick she hoped he'd prevail? My need to know shoved me forward and I bolted to the bed, leveling my gaze on the newly born vampire. As his jade-colored eyes locked with mine, I shuffled back at arm's length. I did exactly what I said I wouldn't do. "Where's Rick? I wanna see Rick!"

An inner glow lit inside his eyes. "This body is mine now. As I recall, you opted out."

Hypatia whipped her head in his direction. "Lucius, answer him!"

He drew in a breath, then let it fly with a loud huff. "Yes, dear." Was he mocking her? He transferred his disfavor to me. "I did nothing. When I opened these eyes, I sensed I was alone. There was no battle, not even a tug-of-war. Perhaps he simply conceded."

"No, he wouldn't just give up." I lunged forward and grabbed him by the shoulders, shaking him as hard as I could. "Rick, you said you were a tough son of a bitch. Prove it! Fight back, dammit!"

"That's enough," Kohath bellowed with authority as he pulled me off, depositing me into Cleopatra's arms. "Take him outside, now!"

She whisked me into the hallway before I had a chance to put up a fight. Seconds later, Kohath barged out the door, then Jim Morrison. I leveled my gaze on them, clenching my fists, ready to wreak havoc, then my chin started to tremble.

Damn it, no way was I gonna cry! My emotions just spilled out, and I couldn't fight the angry sobs crushing my chest.

My legs crumbled and I sank to my knees, balling.

"Believe, Brandon." Cleopatra's voice filled my ears. "It's too soon for claims of victory." Her arm came around my shoulder and she lifted me to my feet. "Say it."

I looked into her convincing eyes, and with one continuous nod, I said, "I believe."

"You must be patient as well," Jim Morrison added.

"I will, I promise. But now what?"

"It's time for you and your sister to return home," Kohath butted in with that authoritative voice of his. "Your journey has ended."

I stumbled backward, shaking my head. "Leave? I can't leave. I won't. Rick needs me. I have to stay for him."

"Here, knowledge, strength, and generosity will surround Rick. When, and if, he's ready, he will come to you," Jim Morrison offered up, trying his hand at fatherly advice. "Your role now is one of patience."

"I can wait, but here with Rick. I can't abandon him after what he did for me." I cut a firm hand through the air. "I'm staying."

"But for how long, Brandon? Days, weeks, months?" Cleopatra pointed out. "Would Rick want you to put your life or your sister's life on hold?"

Cleopatra was the voice of reason, and I didn't like it, but she had a point. I had to think about Lindsey. She needed Mom and Dad. Hell, I needed Mom and Dad. This was the journey Rick chose, and I had to wait out the outcome, but I needed a favor. I set my sights on Cleopatra, hoping for her compassion as I asked, "Worst-case scenario, let's say it's been a year and I haven't heard from Rick, will you come find me and tell me what's happened?"

Her flawless pale face showed no trace of emotion. "Yes, of course."

I peered into her jewel-like eyes, trying to gauge her sincerity. I couldn't, but I wanted to believe her. I needed to believe her. "Then I can go home."

"I'm proud of you, son," Kohath said, gripping my shoulder. "Once we've erased your memories of our Haven and the events which led you here, your lives will be as they once were."

"What?" I shook my head so hard, I teetered backward. "You're not taking anything from me. After everything I've been through—the pain, the hurt, the fear, the lies—I've *earned* those memories."

"I understand your emotional—"

Laughter flew out of my mouth. "There's no way in hell you understand what I've been through, what my family's been through. What Rick's been through. I won't let you take that away from me."

His voice softened. "We can remove all you have suffered as though it had never happened."

I, in turn, raised my voice. "Are you gonna make everyone forget? My mom, my dad, my sister, my teacher, my classmates, my friends, the doctors, the nurses? No. Fix it another way. Let us start over. Something, anything, but you're not messing with my head."

Cleopatra came between us and forced Kohath to face her. "Brandon has Hypatia's blood inside him, and now mine. Compelling him to forget is only temporary. The vampire blood will fight the compulsion and allow his memories to return." She glanced at me, then gave Kohath her full attention. "And he is right. There are far too many humans involved. We can meet with The Council to discuss alternative solutions. For now, let's send Brandon and Lindsey on their way and with their memories intact.

"I agree with Isis," Jim Morrison said, hooking an arm around her shoulder and giving her a kiss on the cheek.

Kohath crossed his arms and heaved a sigh. "Of course, you do. However, I did neglect to consider the mortals comprised. Compulsion is unrealistic, and a meeting of The Council is necessary." He set his sights on me. "You will leave, whole."

My brain wrestled with whether to thank him or not. I mean, I had every right to my memories, but then, he was an all-powerful, ancient vampire and head of his own council. He could've done whatever the hell he wanted, so it was probably best to show my appreciation. "Thank you."

"I'm happy to help. Now, let's get you and your sister home." He turned to the duo. "Isis, Osiris, escort Brandon back to his room and instruct Caleb and Margarete to glide them safely home."

"Consider it done," Jim Morrison confirmed. Locking his arm around me, he bolted.

A whoosh of air blasted my face, then the hallway blurred. Distorted shapes zoomed past us, but from the echo of metal, we'd hit the stairwell. A creak of a second door ended the relay race, and I was back in our room, where my gaze fell on Lindsey, sandwiched by Caleb and Margarete. Lindsey rushed forward, stopping inches away, her eyes wide and locked on mine. "Did you see Rick?"

Her words slammed into my heart, setting off a sob bomb. Rick was gone, and I couldn't change that. I had to survive, but how? As Lindsey's arms came around me and squeezed tight, I unloaded all my pain.

"It's okay," she whispered, her own tears strangling her voice. "We're gonna be okay."

We clung to each other forever it seemed before I let her go. I brushed a sleeve across my face, erasing the tears.

"We should go," Margarete urged, her voice filling my ears.

"Chop, chop," Caleb added, clapping his hands.

As I turned from Lindsey, only Margarete and Caleb remained in the room. Jim Morrison and Cleopatra had vanished. They'd done their part, so there was no point in them sticking around for goodbyes. I looked back at Lindsey. "Ready to go home?"

"So ready."

CHAPTER 16

The metal taste of copper sliding over my tongue jarred my eyes open. Caleb loomed over me, his open wrist pressed to my lips. I shoved him backward and scurried to my feet, bumping into Lindsey who was already on her feet, wiping blood off her mouth. I grabbed her shoulders. "Are you okay?" Before she could answer, I spun around, skimming the street. "Where are we?"

"We're on Dresher, a few blocks from your home," Margarete announced, pointing to the street sign.

"Had to divert," Caleb smirked. "Seems the police have an interest in your whereabouts."

I sagged against Lindsey. "We're home."

Lindsey shivered. "Just got home vibes."

"I suspect you can find your way from here?" Margarete surmised.

I glanced at her over Lindsey's shoulder and nodded.

Without another word, Margarete and Caleb catapulted upward, vanishing into the night.

"C'mon. Let's go home." Lindsey grabbed my hand and tugged me forward. "I'm grateful you're you again, but I'm so over the whole vampire thing."

I wasn't. Things with Rick were up in the air, and until I had answers, vampires were my BFFs. For Lindsey, I veered the conversation elsewhere. "Ya know, we're in a shitload of trouble, right? Mom and Dad are gonna be pissed."

She gave me a playful nudge. "Well, more you than me."

I nudged back. "You threatened to tell if I didn't bring you."

"They won't see it that way."

I offered her my *Forest Gump* sneer, something I picked up after Mom forced me and Lindsey to sit through her favorite DVD, like hundreds of times. "I shouldn't have let you come. I put you in danger." My voice cracked, then I squeaked out, "I'm sorry."

Her eyes turned glassy, then she threw her arms around me and hugged me. "I love you, Brandon. You're the best brother ever."

"Love you too, Lins, even though you're a major pain," I teased.

She gawked at me. "Hey!"

I laughed and held up my hands. "Kidding."

"Better be."

"Seriously, though, they'll probably ground us for the rest of our lives."

"Yeah, I know."

As we turned onto our street, my heart fluttered in my throat. The moment of truth was just a few houses down. At least I wouldn't have to endure our parents' wrath alone. "Thanks for believing in me." She smiled up at me, and it was so genuine, I stopped to hug her once more.

"You're my brother. Of course, I believe in you."

"Brandon and Lindsey Cass?" A male voice popped up out of nowhere. I turned toward the authoritative voice and sized up an ashy-haired man dressed in a suit, minus the jacket, quickly approaching. "Are you Brandon and Lindsey Cass?"

"Yes," I answered, feeling my stomach sink.

He hooked a strong arm around me and Lindsey, whisking us toward our home, shouting, "Martinez, Shultz, I found them!"

Footsteps hammered the sidewalk, then more suits appeared. An armor of bodies surrounded me and Lindsey, like they were protecting the president, shoving and pushing us all the way through our front door. It slammed with a thud, but not loud enough to mask the heightened voices coming from the living room. Two of those voices I knew well— Mom and Dad. I gulped down a nervous breath as the suits shuffled me and Lindsey toward our parents. Lindsey had that saucer-eyed expression of terror etched into her face. I should've said something to her, but there wasn't a simple fix.

Whatever we had coming, we'd have to suffer through it.

The suits deposited Lindsey and me in the center of the living room, as if presenting a trophy. Mom and Dad had the moment of unhinged jaws—the kind that dangled wide open for several seconds before snapping shut. Mom sprang off the sofa first, with Dad right behind her. Their arms flung around us as Mom wailed and Dad blubbered, squishing me and Lindsey inside a group hug.

Mom finally broke away, then held us at arm's length, her eyes darting back and forth between us. "Thank God you're safe." More squeals pierced my eardrums, then her arms fell to her sides and a shiver gripped her entire body.

Dad hung on, kissing the top of Lindsey's head, then mine. "Thank God is right."

"Excuse me, Mr. Cass," the ashy-haired suit interrupted.

"We need to ask the kids a few questions."

Dad nodded but kept a hand on both me and Lindsey.

The suit motioned to the sofa. "Why don't you both take a seat?"

A pained look spread across Dad's face as he let go. Lindsey and I claimed opposite ends of the couch. I snatched up a pillow, hugging it close to my chest, then snuck a peek at Lindsey. She sat perfectly still, with her hands resting on her knees.

Someone hit up my dad's cell before the suit could get out his question. My dad swiped the screen, then waved it off. "My boss. I'll call him back."

The ashy-haired suit forced a smile. He gave it a good solid minute before turning his focus on Lindsey and me. "Brandon, Lindsey, my name is Detective Frost." He gave a nod to the two suits on his right, a freckle-faced stocky man, and a woman with spiky short hair and glasses. "This is Detective Shultz and Detective Martinez." He then gestured to the suits on his left, a bald man with a full beard, and a man who had one of those faces you'd forget the moment he was out of sight. "This is Detective Locket and Detective Freeman."

I made a mental note, Frost: Ash, Shultz: Freckles, Martinez: Glasses, Locket: Baldy, and Freeman: Faceless. "Can you tell us about where you've been for the past six days?"

"A few places." I laughed. "It was kind of a road trip."

Lindsey fired off a direct response. "We took a bus to Castle Beach."

Ash tapped a pen against a notepad. "Castle Beach? Why there?"

Lindsey shrugged. "No reason."

"There's always a reason," Glasses spoke up. "Who came up with the destination of Castle Beach?"

"I did," I said, crossing my arms. "But you probably already know that if you searched my computer."

Ash chuckled. "We did. We also have several witnesses to your whereabouts, as well as Rick Miles, who was seen with the two of you." He paused and scratched his head. "Why didn't you take your cell phones with you?"

I shot a brief glance Mom and Dad's way, then locked my gaze on Ash. "Cell phones can be tracked. I needed space and time to think. Plus, I left a note for my parents."

"We read the note, and confirmed you wrote it. What did you need time to think about?"

"What difference does it make?" I threw back at Ash.

Ash opened his mouth, but the chime of my dad's cell silenced him. He tossed a hefty scowl my dad's way.

"Sorry, the boss again." Dad ditched his cell, sliding it across the coffee table. "It's on vibrate now."

Ash ignored my dad as his beady sights had shifted to me. "We've done our research, Brandon. You kept it clean, paid everything with cash, but still, we were able to trace transactions, leading us to the Sleeptime Lodge, then nothing." A frown swallowed up his forehead. "Was it Rick's idea to pay in cash and leave your phones at home? Doesn't seem like something teenagers would come up with on their own."

Lindsey and I stole a glance at each other, but kept our mouths shut.

"Answer the question, please."

"It was Rick's idea," I admitted. "But I went along with it. It made sense."

"I went along with it too," Lindsey added.

Ash didn't let up. "Why the secrecy? Why didn't you want to be found?"

"I already told you, I needed space and—"

"Time to think," he finished for me as his probing eyes stared me down.

Freckles stepped up to the plate and added his two cents. "Rick seems to be the mastermind behind this trip. Was he running away from something or someone? Where is he now?"

Why were they so focused on Rick? The spotlight should've been on me. "Running? He wasn't running." "But where is he?"

"Um...I don't know. He decided not to come back."

Ash lifted a single eyebrow. "And he let the two of you came back on your own?"

What the hell was wrong with this guy? "Why not?"

He leveled his gaze on me. "He wasn't holding you against your will?"

I let my laughter fly. "Where are you coming up with this stuff? No."

"Obviously, you've never met Rick," Lindsey shot back with a sneer.

"Brandon, Lindsey, watch your tone," Mom scolded.

"These are detectives you're talking to."

Lame ones, but I kept that to myself. "Yes, Mom." "Yes, Mom," Lindsey echoed.

Dad pinched his lips together, then grinded out, "I should've listened to my gut. Rick put ideas into my son's head. I should've never let him into our home."

"That's your version," I corrected, enlightening him, "but not the truth."

"Brandon!" Mom snapped.

"Hold on, Mr. and Mrs. Cass," Glasses interjected. "Frost is getting somewhere. Let him finish his questioning."

Dad held his hands up in a submissive manner. "Okay, okay. It's just, these are our kids."

"We understand," Glasses sympathized, placing a hand on Dad's shoulder.

Mom's face looked paler than a vampire's, and Dad's muscles strained against his skin as Rick's character was getting hammered. The cops blamed him. My parents blamed him. They'd kicked Rick out. Neither trusted him. Had they planted the seed that Rick was dangerous? Was that why the cops were all over him?

Ash's voice barged inside my head. "What was Rick's role on this trip?"

I blinked, then focused on the detective. "Role? I don't get it."

"Was he the mastermind behind the trip or just tagged along for support?"

I pinched my lips together, then shelved the sarcasm for Mom. "We planned everything together."

"Did you ever split up along the way or were you together 24/7?" His gaze narrowed, and his words came out in a low, merciless tone. "We know the three of you shared a hotel room. Did he force himself on the two of you?"

Mom let out a strangled gasp. Dad sat still, a dazed look claiming his face.

I fixed the coldest, hardest glare I could make on Ash. "No, he did not!"

"Force?" Lindsey asked, a frown tugging at her brows.

My naïve little sister didn't get it, but I had. My immediate response hadn't done Rick justice, but Ash's question caught me off guard. I popped off the couch and blurted out, "That's just sick." I whipped around and confronted my parents. "Is that what you think? Did you plant that crap in their heads?"

Mom trembled, then latched onto Dad, shaking her head. "No, of course not."

Lindsey's eyes widened, then she lobbed an accusing glare toward the detectives. "Oh my God! Are you kidding me? Rick isn't a monster."

Dad cut an unyielding hand through the air. "That's it. This interrogation is over." He shooed the suits toward the door. "My kids are back home and safe. That's all that matters to us."

Ash stood his ground and pushed back. "Mr. Cass, there are many unanswered questions about Rick Miles. Your children could help us with that."

Dad yanked the door wide open. "You'll have to find those answers elsewhere. Now, it's late and my kids need to get to bed."

Glasses ushered her fellow suits out the door, then stopped and gave Dad and Mom a nod. "We're glad your kids are home. Thank you for your time, Mr. and Mrs. Cass."

"You're welcome," Dad replied before closing the door with a firm hand, then leaning against it and letting out an exasperated breath.

Lindsey bounced over and hugged him. "That was awesome, Dad!"

"Ditto," I seconded, sidestepping toward the stairs. "Gonna hit my bed and crash."

"Sit your butts back down!" Dad barked, using his drill sergeant voice. "I want the truth, not some lame version of it—the whole truth."

"Whatever that may be," Mom added, sounding as hard-nosed as Dad.

Lindsey bolted first, then me as we scampered over to the couch. Dad took a wide stance directly in front of us, flashing a defiant stare. Mom stood at his side, a softer expression framing her face. "Start talking," he ordered, crossing his arms.

"I already know you won't believe me," I accused, then raised my voice, rattling off, "Because this whole time, I've been telling you the truth and you've refused to believe me!"

"Brandon's right," Lindsey chimed in. "You didn't believe him, so why would it be any different now?"

Dad held his hands up in an apologetic manner. "Okay, calm down." He glanced at Mom. "I admit we haven't been the most approachable, but considering the recent circumstances, we've decided to come at this with an open mind."

I focused on Mom. If we were sharing, she also had a story to tell. "Then Mom needs to go first."

Dad did a double take. "Diane?"

Mom closed her eyes and heaved a sigh. "There's something I've never told you, Mike." Her eyes opened, then locked on Dad. "At Brandon's birth, something happened... something strange...something I can't explain." She pressed her lips together as a somber expression drained the color from her face. "There was a girl in the delivery room. Do you remember me shouting for her to get out?"

Dad flinched his head back slightly. "You were shouting at everyone. You were in pain."

"I was in pain," Mom agreed, "but I'll never forget how she fixated her extraordinary eyes on me."

I could relate as to how Dad slanted his body away from Mom. She'd freaked me out too when she'd dropped her bombshell on me.

"There was no one there, Diane. It had to have been the drugs."

Mom's voice weakened as she divulged, "The girl wasn't alone...something came with her. She made it enter Brandon." Mom locked her gaze on Dad, then clenched her fists. "When I screamed 'Give me my baby,' you all thought I was crazy. I could see it in your eyes." She pursed her lips, squeezing the blood out of them. "But I wasn't! She was there. Something was with her, and it changed Brandon!"

Dad's face morphed into a "what the hell" expression as he stared at Mom.

"Eve confirmed it," I added, endorsing Mom's words.

Dad's gaze slowly transferred to me. "Eve?"

Mom's hand fluttered before it landed on her chest. She forced a laugh. "Rick's friend, a medium."

I thought Dad's jaw was gonna hit the floor. "You took our son to a psychic?"

"We couldn't tell you, Dad," Lindsey spoke up. "Everything's black and white with you."

Dad grew paler by the minute, but he'd asked for the truth, so I laid it on thick. "You and Mom kicked Rick out because of the whole vampire thing. Yeah, he suggested it, but he'd seen what I'd done, and Eve confirmed it. She told me of an entity planted inside me, that it would provide the answers. I just had to let it lead me, and that's what I did...

what Rick did." Dad wagged a finger at me, but I kept going. "A vampire chatroom led me to Bloodthirst, a vampire club.

The trip to Castle Beach was supposed to be just Rick and me. Then, Lindsey happened."

"I made Brandon take me," Lindsey admitted, dipping her chin to her chest. "I threatened to tell if he didn't. And we saw things..." A shiver ran through her. "Inexplicable things.

Things you can't unsee, things that couldn't possibly be real."

I hooked an arm around her. She came clean, for me, and I loved her for it.

"I can't...I don't..." Mom stammered. "I don't even know what to say."

Dad slipped his arm around Mom, pulling her close. "I think we're both at a loss for words."

I watched my parents' faces slip into these bleak, unfocused, faraway gazes, and wondered if I should say more. "Do you want me to continue?"

Dad gave a curt nod. "No, no, we need to hear. We need to know what happened." "Mom?"

"Yes, keep going," she answered, latching onto Dad's arm.

I drew in a long breath, then released it before continuing. "We met a bunch of vampires, so yeah, they're like totally friggin' real," I preached, enlightening my parents. "The vampires at Bloodthirst knew the girl Mom saw, but she wasn't just a girl, she's a vampire, and what she stuck inside me was the soul of her vampire boyfriend."

Mom turned into this unnaturally quiet person who kept swallowing, and Dad's forehead crinkled up into one big frown.

"She had this crazy idea that I'd just let her turn me into a vampire so her vampire boyfriend could be reborn. Of course, I said hell no. She freaked out, and that's when they took us to this council of vampires, who looked like ancient monks dressed in robes, but it wasn't until they brought in these two vampire gods, who could've been doubles for Jim Morrison and Cleopatra, that they came up with a plan to rid the vampire's soul from my body."

"It was insane," Lindsey blurted out, interrupting me. "Like a movie or a fairy tale, only it was all real. I'll never forget it, ever!"

I held a hand in front of Lindsey. "Let me finish." I focused again on Mom and Dad, who were hanging onto each other, gazes clouding, looking like I'd completely lost my mind. "So, the plan was to find another host to transfer the vampire's soul in to." My voice lost its power, and I trembled.

Lindsey's arm came around me, and she whispered, "It's okay."

In one gulp, I swallowed my grief, then forced out the rest. "That person was Rick. He offered to risk his life to save mine, and he did. Their plan worked. I got my life back, but Rick, he's...he's battling for his."

Mom's chin quivered, then she turned away, pressing her face into Dad's chest. Dad let go of Mom, letting his arm dangle at his side. "This story is far too bizarre for you to have made the whole thing up. I see that now. We were wrong," he mumbled, then cleared his throat and said it with conviction, "We were *wrong*. We should have listened. I'm deeply sorry, son."

Mom and Lindsey started bawling. I slumped into the couch and just stared. I couldn't get out a response, my lips forming silent words. Dad never admitted to being wrong. That had to have been super hard for him. I pulled Lindsey up and dragged her with me over to Mom and Dad. We threw our arms around them, and I sagged against Dad, spewing out tears. "I love you, Dad, Mom, Lindsey."

"Love you, Brandon," Dad murmured, kissing the top of my head, then Lindsey's. "Love you, princess."

Mom smothered my face and Lindsey's with soft kisses. "I love my babies so much."

"Love you guys," Lindsey blubbered.

Dad scrubbed a hand over his face, wiping off his tears, then held me and Lindsey at arm's length. "I understand why you did what you did, but running off like that was not acceptable. We have rules in this house where you're accountable for your actions."

Oh no, here it comes. Grounded. Damn, I thought for sure we'd skated Dad's wrath. I drew my mouth into a thin line, waiting for our sentencing.

Lindsey popped off with, "Nothing could be worse than the punishment we've already been through." She stared up at Dad with her big green eyes. "Time served, Dad?"

He released us to cross his arms over his chest and huff. He gave us a good long once-over, then looked to Mom.

"Diane?"

Mom's gaze ping-ponged between me and Lindsey, then shot to Dad. "What would we punish them for? Searching for answers? Answers we should've helped them with?" She fluttered her hands in the air. "All I care about is that they're home."

Dad pursed his lips, as if weighing his options, then let out a hefty sigh. He nodded in agreement as he said, "Time served."

I high-fived Lindsey, then shoved my hands in my pockets and rocked back and forth on my heels. "Ah. Thanks, Dad."

Lindsey reached up and kissed his cheek. "Thanks, Dad, and I promise never to do anything stupid again."

I held up my hand. "Ditto."

He wagged a finger at us. "I'm holding the two of you to that commitment." Dad's cell vibrated against the coffee table for the sixth time. "Must be an emergency. Let me see what he wants." He scooped up his cell and vanished down the hall.

Mom wrapped an arm around me and Lindsey. "I've never been so scared"—her voice cracked with emotion—"then so thankful in my life. I'm never going to let the two of you out my sight again, ever."

"This is your fault, Brandon," Lindsey whined.

"If you'd stayed home," I fired back with a sneer, "you wouldn't have to deal, so it's kind of your fault too."

"Hey now," Mom intervened. "I'm your mother. I have a right to be protective or I could just ground you." "I'm good with protection," I announced.

Lindsey nodded at a hundred miles an hour. "Yeah, me too."

Dad wandered in with a distant look in his eyes. "I've been transferred to Seattle. Frank's got me on a plane tomorrow."

Mom gasped. "What?"

Lindsey rushed between Mom and Dad, her eyes bulging. "Seattle?"

I stood right where I was. Sounded like a Kohath and team fix to me.

CHAPTER 17

Mom lifted the lid to her spaghetti sauce, and a potent whiff of fresh tomato, garlic, and basil got between me and my algebra. I slapped the book closed and jokingly pounded my head against the white marble island of Mom's dreams. "You're killing me. I'm trying to study here."

Mom's rich laughter filled the room. "I'll take that as a compliment." She glanced at the kitchen clock. "Oh, my heavens, I forgot about Lindsey." Stirring the sauce and dredging up more mouthwatering flavors, she said, "Your sister is at the school library. Can you please go pick her up?"

I wilted onto the barstool and sighed. "Since when did I become Lindsey's personal chauffeur?"

Mom arched a single brow. "Since your father and I bought you that SUV."

"Hey, six months of training with Dad and his"—I did my best Dad impression—"whoa, slow down. Check the rearview mirror. You're too close. Keep your eyes on the road. Oh, and let's not forget his imaginary foot break." I crossed my arms. "I think I earned that SUV."

Mom snorted. "I just got a visual—clenched jaw, eyes wide, foot jammed into the floor..." She hugged her sides, cackling.

"Yep, that's Dad."

She waved her hands in front of her, took a few deep breaths and reclaimed her composure. "You've got a point, but I still need you to go get your sister."

I sprouted my negotiating grin. "On one condition."

Now it was her turn to cross her arms. "Which is?"

"Spaghetti's not the same without your cheesy garlic bread."

She jutted out her hand, and I slapped mine against hers, giving it a firm shake. "You strike a hard bargain, but you've got yourself a deal. One loaf of cheesy garlic bread coming right up." She shooed me away. "Now, go get your sister."

I dug my keys out of my pocket. "Be back in a few."

"No diversions," Mom yelled as I trudged through the living room. "Dinner's served when your dad gets home."

"Got it." I headed out the door and into the dreary gray of Seattle. The normal steady drizzle fell from the sky. "Doesn't this stuff have an off switch?" I mumbled, pulling my hoodie over my head and climbing into my RAV4. I hadn't seen the sun in eight months. In L.A., sunshine was my shadow, following me around wherever I went. Here, we got rain. As I backed out into the street, I reminded myself that the move was a good thing. Nobody knew us here. We didn't have to hide or explain the past. We could relax, be ourselves, and move forward with our new normal.

I flipped on the radio and the Chainsmokers' "Don't Let Me Down" annihilated the justifying demons inside my head. I cranked up the volume, blasting tunes the entire way to the school. As I swung into a parking space and killed the engine, the memory of granting our school its name flashed inside my head. Mom had brought Lindsey, who had just turned 15, and me to register. She had a clipboard in her lap, shuffling through a ton of paperwork, when I'd leaned over and whispered, "This school looks like one of your red velvet cakes, magnified by a thousand." Laughter had flown out of her mouth and the pen had gone airborne too, hitting the receptionist in the head. Me and Lindsey had twisted around in our chairs, stifling our glee as best we could. Mom had rushed over to the girl and gushed about how sorry she was, while sneaking a sneer at me. Drizzle scattering across the windshield pulled me back to the present. I shook my head, gazing at school. "It still looks like a huge red velvet cake."

I knew Lindsey wouldn't be on time. She'd become hooked on books, and the library was her thing. Maybe it was her coping mechanism to keep the scary images from creeping back into her brain. She never talked about what had happened, but our vampire journey had changed her. The self-centered, "it's all about me" Lindsey was gone. Her nightmares started a few weeks after we'd moved to Seattle. At least once a week, in the middle of the night, she'd rush into my room with this haunted look. I'd mumble, "Did you have the dream again?"

She'd grip the new permanent fixture around her throat, a cross pendant, and whispered, "Yes. I think something's in my room. Can you please come check?"

I'd stumbled half-awake into her room, check her closet, under her bed, and behind her shower curtain, then I'd shake my head. "There's nothing here, Lins."

She'd clutch the cross tighter. "You're sure?"

"Yes. Now, go back to sleep."

She'd latch onto my arm. "Can you stay, just until I fall asleep?"

I'd flop down on the chaise in the corner of her room, and she'd cover me with a throw blanket.

I couldn't blame her. It changed me too. Vampire blood lived inside of me—Hypatia's, Caleb's, and Cleopatra's. I didn't have to wonder if something was in my room. I knew when it was, but I'd been the instigator, reaching out to Cleopatra for news. She'd never show herself, only used her voice. The temperature had always dropped, spreading an icy chill down my arms. My second clue had been my own breath hovering in front of my eyes. I'd peer into my room and call out, "Has he remembered anything?" Her message never changed. It was always, "Give him time." The last time I'd heard those words was over a month ago.

The drizzle suddenly stopped. I pushed the car door open and stepped into the scent of musty rainwater. I glanced toward the library; still no sign of Lindsey. It was looking like I'd have to go get her when she appeared on the walkway, books tucked inside her arms, eyes cast downward, dragging her feet along in protest for having to leave the library. "Lins," I called out, waving at her.

Her head popped up and a smile spread on her lips. She waved back, taking larger strides and quickening her pace.

Across the street, a flicker of light hit the corner of my eye. I squinted, peering into the thick cluster of trees lining the opposite side of the street. Two pairs of glimmering, jewel-like eyeballs gazed back. My skin prickled as the tiny hairs on my arms lifted. Those were vampire eyes! If Rick had won the battle, Cleopatra would've signaled me. She'd promised, and I'd gotten zilch. No way was I hanging around to find out who the orbs belonged to. My gaze darted to Lindsey, and I wildly waved her over. "Lindsey, get in the car, now!" I dashed to her side, then latched onto her arm, pulling her forward. "We gotta go."

She rooted her feet to the ground, resisting. "What's wrong?"

I couldn't tell her. She'd freak out. "Um...we're gonna be late for dinner. Mom and Dad will be pissed."

She yanked her arm back. "Chill. We'll make it."

I pressed my hand on her back, hurrying her along. "Yeah, well, they'll blame me if were late, so c'mon."

"You're acting super weird."

"Am I?" I asked, my gaze darting around as I fumbled for the door handle. My fingers brushed against icy flesh. I shot a look over my shoulder into Hypatia's ocean-blue eyes. I gasped out loud, sagging against the car door. "Jesus, Hypatia, you scared the crap out of me."

"No, no, no," Lindsey uttered, backing away. "Not again."

I grabbed Lindsey's arm and tucked her behind me. "It's okay, Lins. Hypatia won't hurt us." My gaze shifted to the vampire. "What do you want?" I pointed to the trees. "And who's with you?"

Hypatia plastered that superior look on her face. "If I wanted something, I'd just take it. I'm not here for me." Her look softened. "He's remembering. I think he's...Rick is fighting to come back."

I shook all over. I'd hoped for this moment every minute of every day, prayed even, but Cleopatra was supposed to warn me. Why hadn't she? "Wh—" Tears choked my voice, then I shoved them back down with one swallow. "Why do you think that? What's he done? And why didn't Cleo—Isis—warn me?"

"Isis and Osiris are visiting their son. She's unaware of the recent events," Hypatia causally explained. She glanced toward the trees, then back at me, pausing for several seconds before continuing. "At his request, I took him to Los Angeles, where he stood in front of your old home until the sun threatened to rise. He turned to me and said, "I tutored a boy who lived in this house.""

An uncontrollable sob exploded out of me, and I fell against Lindsey. She steadied me, then hugged me. I cried in her arms forever it seemed before I pulled away to face Hypatia. Sweeping tears off my face, I said, "I want to see him."

Hypatia slid closer, narrowing the gap between us. "He's struggling with his identity. One wrong word from you, and I'll whisk him away."

I placed my hand over my heart. "I love him. He's like a brother to me. I won't say the wrong thing."

Her gaze flipped to Lindsey. "And you?"

Lindsey's voice was barely a whisper. "I won't either."

Hypatia vanished, then I grabbed Lindsey's hand. "I'm nervous."

She laced her fingers with mine, squeezing tight. "Me too."

A whoosh of air whipped through my hair as Hypatia reappeared. This time, with Rick on her arm. He was Rick2.0, rebuilt like one of the *X-Men*; wheelchair and scars—gone. His dark brown glowing eyes locked with mine. The last time I'd looked into them, they were the color of jade.

Lindsey let go of my hand, shaking her head and staring.

His gaze remained fixed on me. Every few seconds, he'd tilt his head side to side and squint like he couldn't figure me out. He needed to come to his own conclusions as to who I was, so I kept my mouth shut. Nobody spoke, we all just stood there. It was a standoff of glares. After a good five minutes, he broke the silence. "You're the boy, the boy I tutored." I sucked in a much-needed breath. "Yes." "I'm his sister," Lindsey murmured.

His eyes flashed to her, then returned to me. "As I remember, there was something wrong with you, yes?"

Again, I kept my answer simple. "Yes, there was."

He let go of Hypatia's arm and stepped closer. "And I helped you."

I gave him a slight smile. "You did."

The squint returned, swallowing up his forehead. "What exactly did I do?"

I looked to Hypatia, and she came between us, brushing the back of her hand down his cheek. "What do *you* think you did?"

"I—I don't know." He tapped his knuckles on top of his head. "The answer's there, but I can't get it out."

"Take your time, love. There's no hurry."

He gazed at her for some time before finally turning to me. "Are you better now?"

A laugh slipped out before I answered. "Much better. I'm me again."

He pointed to himself. "Did I help with that?"

"Very much so."

He gathered his brows together, then released them. "I have this warmth around my heart when I look at you, like we're brothers."

Sobs gripped my chest, then I shuddered. "We had a close friendship, like brothers."

"You believed him," Lindsey spoke up, "when others wouldn't."

He snapped his fingers. "I remember. There was this struggle within you, but your parents didn't believe you."

Lindsey snickered. "And they didn't like you, especially my dad."

Hypatia leveled her gaze at Lindsey.

"Lins, don't," I cautioned.

"No, it's okay. I want you to speak freely," he said with a confident nod, before cocking his head. "I think I do remember. They kicked me out because..." He squeezed his eyes shut and stood completely still, then slowly opened them, letting them grow wider and wider. "I took you to see Eve. Ha!" he blurted out, spinning around in a circle. "They thought I was putting thoughts into your head and kicked me out." "Yes!" I shouted.

A pained look spread across his face, then his hand gripped his stomach. A guttural cough flew out of his mouth, then another, and another. He stumbled backward and doubled over. Hypatia rushed to his side, laying her hands on him. "What is it? What's wrong?"

He shooed her away, then collapsed to all fours. She stood by his side, trembling, her eyes darting about. I pushed Lindsey into the car and ran to his side. The hacking grew into explosive retching, shaking his whole body. Gray flakes flew out of his mouth, fluttering like baby birds, then fell to the ground. A pile of countless flakes lay under the moonlight, pulsating. His gagging lessened, a flake here or there, then nothing. He struggled for a few breaths before regaining a normal, calm rhythm. He slowly sat up, a dazed look in his eyes.

I gently placed my hand on his shoulder. "Are you okay?"

His eyes found mine, an inner light shining bright within them. He gripped my shoulder. "Brandon?"

My chin quivered as I bobbed my head. "Yeah, it's me."

He pounded his fist on his chest and burst out laughing. "It's Rick! Told ya I was a tough son of a bitch."

I hugged him with all my might, tears streaming down my face. "Yeah, you did."

"Look!" Hypatia shrieked.

I followed her finger back to the pile of junk that came out of Rick. The gray flakes were crumbling into white chalky ash, a few inched apart, separating themselves in a desperate attempt to stay alive. I scrambled to my feet, backing away. Rick stood tall, glaring down at the flecks of white. Hypatia collapsed to her knees and let out a gasp. My gaze ping-ponged between their conflicting expressions, then I got it—I knew. The gray flakes that spewed from Rick had been Lucius. Rick had won the battle. Lucius was dying.

Rick knelt next to Hypatia, placing his hand on her back. She let her head fall against his shoulder. "It's over," she muttered.

"Rick?" I questioned, edging toward them.

He held up a hand, holding me off. His arms came around Hypatia, pulling her close and she clung to him, wailing. Lindsey snuck up behind me, tapping my shoulder. "What's going on?"

"Damn it, Lindsey, I told you to stay in the car!" I snapped.

I wasn't her focus, Hypatia was. "I couldn't sit alone, listening to that."

I wrapped an arm around her and sighed. "Lucius is dead."

Her breath seemed to hitch in her chest, then she latched onto my arm. "So, does that mean Rick is Rick?"

I'd never been so at peace with the world as I'd been in that moment. "Yes, it does."

She squealed, then threw her arms around me and bounced up and down. "Oh my God, oh my God!" Her delight faded away as she set her sights on Hypatia. "I feel sorry for her."

"Me too."

Hypatia let go of Rick, then slowly pushed to her feet. Rick rose with her. She looked up at him, brushing tears from her face as she said, "Saving him was my life. How do I move forward? I have no right to ask you to stay, yet I'm asking."

He tucked a strand of her hair behind her ear. "I'm not going anywhere." Then he kissed her.

I covered Lindsey's eyes with my hand. "For adults only."

She elbowed me, then pushed my hand away. "Like you're an adult?"

I waved her away. "Whatever." "Whatever," she mimicked.

"Knock it off, children," Rick teased, walking toward us with a subdued Hypatia on his arm.

Lindsey bounced up to him and gave him a big hug. "Rick! I'm so happy you're back!"

He tousled her hair. "Me too, me too." He turned to Hypatia. "Can I have a moment alone with Brandon?"

"Of course." Hypatia replied.

Rick led me a few feet away from Lindsey and Hypatia. A serious expression sucked the joy from his face. "This has to be goodbye, Brandon."

His words hit like a fist to the gut. "What? Why?"

He pressed his lips together into a slight grimace. "I have desires, hungers that I can't control. I can't protect you from who I am now."

I waved him off. "No, you would never hurt me."

He laughed. "I wish I had your confidence. I've yet to master these new gifts of mine. I see and hear as a god. My strength surpasses a hundred men. I can destroy everything I touch. The sky is my playground. I can move with the speed of light. My mind is a master of control." He squeezed his eyes shut, then shook his head. "I live by night to avoid the sun." He looked directly at me. "I have to drink blood to survive. I need Hypatia to guide me. Along with her heart, she's offered me her strength and wisdom. She's my family now."

I shifted my weight from foot to foot. He wanted me to just give up? I wouldn't. I couldn't. "I admit I don't know that much about vampires and their lives, but if given the choice, I'd like to stay friends."

Rick gripped my shoulders. "We'll always be friends, man."

"So don't say goodbye!" I cried.

"Brandon, I made a choice to be part of a world that threatens humans." His chin trembled, then stopped. "I have to keep you safe, and to do that, I can't be near you, or let other vampires near you. I did all this so you could be free of vampires and live a normal, happy life."

I pressed my fist against my heart. "And I'm grateful." Tears started falling. I couldn't control them. "You're my best friend. I love you."

He reached out and hugged me, then quickly pulled away. "I love you too, man."

I sucked up the pain, sniffled, then extended my hand.

"Let's make a pact."

He gave me a chin bob. "What kind of pact?"

"A communication pact."

"I'm listening."

I shrugged. "Like texting, hitting up each other's cell, or vampire communication by thought. You could send me a thought message."

Laughter shook his shoulders. "I think I can do that."

"Let's shake on it."

He grabbed my hand, giving it a firm shake. "Pact accepted."

About the Author

Laura Daleo was born and raised in San Diego, California where she majored in Fine Arts at Mesa College. She is best known for her love of animals. She is an animal advocate and shares her home with three humorous Basset Hounds, Stuart, Morgan, and Dexter, her toughest critics. Laura has held positions in several industries, Restaurant, Telecom, Biotech, Research, and Retail.

A creative writing class in junior high sparked her desire to tell stories. Throughout Laura's professional career, she crafted her writing skills by taking courses and by joining writer's critique groups and Writers Digest. She enjoys anything paranormal or fantasy related, and writes in both genres.